On the Line

Branson M. Smith

Hope you enjoy!

– P[signature]

3-30-24

ISBN: 9798871946985
ISBN-13:

Dedicated to the industry, an unrelenting peril of tickets, clientèle, and stressful lunch rushes.
To my family, thank you for always being there.
To Rose, thanks for reading and being my constant muse and salvation.

1

Chapter 1

1

I stood there gazing at the French fries cooking in the basket. My hand rested on the handle, but I was lost and nowhere to be found.

I didn't mean to be here, I didn't plan on a career at this restaurant; but for the last ten years, I have been a dedicated and loyal employee of the Open House Bar and Grill. Where has the time gone?

"Sam. Sam! Samuel!" My coworker on the grill was trying to get my attention and pull me from the depths of my wondering.

I snapped out of it. "Yeah? Sorry, man." I lifted the basket of fries.

Greg was very good at his job running the grill. Older, almost sixty years old, he had been doing this kind of kitchen work since he was able to work at the age of sixteen. I could watch him grill up eight patties at once and he wouldn't even flinch. The lunch rush didn't scare him, and he rarely got food sent back; not even one complaint since I could remember.

"These burgers are about to come up and I need those fries ready."

"Heard." I double checked my tickets to make sure I had the

correct count for the fries.

The fryers were buzzing, the grill sizzling, but in all of this commotion, I didn't feel the same passion I had once felt for cooking years ago. I had to put all my worry and concerns out of my mind right now though—we were right in the middle of lunch service.

Greg started to plate up his hamburger patties and buns. He handed them over to me and I added the fries. I then passed them along to Terry. He was the expediter, and his job was to put the appropriate vegetables on the plates and add ranch dressing on the side if needed.

"Are those burgers almost done?" Jessica, one of the waitresses, asked at the order window. She seemed frustrated and growing impatient.

"They're almost up," Terry said, "Just give us a moment!"

"Don't yell at me," she retorted. "I'm not your mama! You respect me or shut up!"

Terry laughed. "I'm not your mama, but I could be your daddy if you let me."

"Whatever!" she replied, putting up her hand and walking away.

He turned to me. "Do you have that last burger with Swiss and bacon?"

"Swiss?" I asked Greg, my robust partner.

"It's right in front of you."

I hadn't noticed Greg had put it on the stainless-steel table. I lifted the plate and passed it on to Terry.

"My guy," Terry snickered.

I was ready to give up; shoot, I had been ready for the last three years. I was thirty-five with no potential of doing anything else—no skills, no open opportunities to get out from underneath this place. I was at a dead end, and I hated it. My dream was always to perform live on stage as a musician. I had a group, and we were decent, but this area of Texas was no place for aspiring musicians to seize their dreams and make a name for themselves. Just as my life was at a halt at the Open House Bar and Grill, so was my music career; I would never be that rock star I so aspired to be.

2

After the last ticket that I could see coming in for the lunch rush, I told Greg I was going to step out for a smoke. He nodded. I exited the small kitchen and made my way out the back door to the outside to get a breath of fresh air and my nicotine fill. I put the cigarette in my lips and lit the end.

Damn, it's nice to get one in right after the crowd pours into the restaurant and tears the place apart.

I exhaled and looked around the alley. Empty beer cans on the ground, and dumpsters along the sides of the buildings. At least it was quiet. I took in a deep breath this time dragging from my full-flavored cigarette.

Yeah, I'm not gonna be a rock star, or be a professional cook with their own television show, but it could be worse. The only thing that really bothered me, honestly speaking, was that I never met someone who seemed to truly love and care for me—that and I never had kids.

Thinking about the afternoon tasks, however, that I would have to complete before I left work, I knew I needed to make more hamburgers out of scratch, I needed to put up the order that had just come in on the delivery produce truck in its' appropriate places in the walk-in fridge and freezer, breakdown boxes and dump them in the designated trash bin out here to my left and tie up any loose ends so the night shift wouldn't have anything to complain about.

I looked down at the cigarette and it had become nothing more than a butt. It was time to go back inside.

"Hey, are we still on for after work?" Terry asked me as I walked back into the kitchen.

"Every time we go out to a bar, you always want to go to a strip club at the end of the night. And every time I tell you no, it's too much money. I have bills, man. I can't spend $20 on a dance from a stranger. I don't want some chick's funk-ass crotch all over me. It's not my thing. Plus, I can't go home smelling like street hooker because my dad will give me the third degree and will never let up unless I give him every fucking detail of the night and the shenanigans that you got me in to."

"All right. I can understand that," Terry replied.

"Sam," Greg interrupted. "I need my patties whenever you get caught up."

"Sure," I replied.

I finished forming my hamburger patties and filled up the pan. I put them in the walk-in fridge, where I always do in the spot where they always go. I sat up front in the dining area to catch my breath and cool off. I looked down at my phone. Three o'clock. I was off at four.

I could use a beer, but not with Terry. He was too much trouble. He loved women, beer, cocaine, and to live a lot faster than I did. I didn't like that stuff, although I was a musician that used to gig regularly. It wasn't my scene. I preferred to be at home and write my songs in my spare time. It's what brought me joy.

3

I was sitting at the table when Jessica came up and sat down too.

"So, what do you have planned tonight?" she asked.

"Not much," I replied. "I'll probably just go home, check on my dad, and make some dinner."

"Are you still playing music?"

"Yeah, but we're on hiatus right now. The bass player's wife is expecting their second kid so just taking a break so he can figure all of that out."

"Well, that's good," she said.

I could tell she wasn't enthused. Jessica was that air-headed girl who was too pretty for her own good. I always thought she was cute, but I would never hit on her. I doubt she would even reciprocate the gesture. I wasn't even going to try to get shot down, especially at my workplace. I didn't want the humiliation lingering over me. I've been here way too long at this restaurant to ruin the atmosphere for myself. I was comfortable here.

"Did the schedule get sent out yet?" I asked Jessica.

"No, but I think it will come out tonight."

I was ready to clock out and head home. I wanted my afternoon coffee. Thirty minutes until four o'clock. I scrolled through my social media. There were always posts of people getting engaged, married, birthdays, and having brand new babies left and right. I had none of that. I got married once when I was twenty-six, but that was short-lived. Two years of separation, and then it ended in a quick divorce. I had no children. Maybe a few pregnancy scares, and one official paternity test through the courthouse, but none of the kids were mine. The women would always say, "Of course he or she is yours," but they never were. I'm not sure if I was fine with that. I did want kids. I wanted to be a father, but not like that I suppose. Not by a one-night stand. It was just me, a thirty-five-year-old man with schizophrenia in a little apartment and his ailing father. The schizophrenia was difficult sometimes, but I managed. The times seemed bleak. I did love my dad—of course, he was my hero growing up. So now, it was my turn to take care of him. But I wanted more out of life. I wanted more than forty hours at the restaurant never moving up in the chain. I wanted more for myself. I have potential. Well, I *had* potential. I wasn't so sure now.

Terry walked up.

"They hired a new girl." He grinned at me.

"Great," I replied. He kept staring with an ugly smile. "Why do you always do that?"

"What?" He laughed.

"You do that thing where you insinuate another thing and I hate it." I couldn't help but laugh though. I didn't like it when Terry made jokes about the new waitresses. He was always hinting. He was single, like me, but he would try to get laid by the new unsuspecting girl as soon as he could.

"I'm not saying anything," Terry replied. "But I *am saying* Greg said she was hot."

"Greg did not say that."

"Yeah. Yeah, he did. He said she had a fat butt."

"Dude, that's gross."

"You don't like big, fat asses? I know you like big asses. Don't lie."

One thing was for sure— it had been some time since I had sex. I won't deny I look at the waitresses occasionally. I had to. The need to look was buried deep within me. I was programmed as a human-being to look at an ass or two during my shifts. I couldn't help it; just like Terry couldn't help his wild antics and perverse nature. We were people caught up in a world infatuated by sex and lust; we were at its mercy.

"I'd like a cute chick with a personality," I replied.

"Lame," Terry said and chuckled. "Where are your balls? Did you leave them back at home? Does your dad have them? Man, you need to get in touch with your animal side and let the true Sam come out. He's down there somewhere; or maybe he's lost along with your nuts."

"I hate you."

"You too, my friend." He walked back to the kitchen.

4

Good. It was four o'clock and I could leave now. I was ready to get away from this circus.

I got into my car and lit a smoke. I sat there for a moment just staring out of my front window. I wondered how life had slipped away from me these past few years. It didn't help that I had gone to the mental hospital two years ago. I needed help. I was a monster then.

I was diagnosed with schizophrenia when I was twenty-one. There was an incident. I had a nervous break, and it was common for some youth to become schizophrenic between the ages of eighteen and twenty-two. It happened to me. I had spent the last ten years and some change figuring out my place and trying to control my mind as best as I could, but two years ago, I lost my shit again when I found out this girl that I was dating had been cheating on me most of our time together. I guess I had just lost my mind once again and the only place anyone could think of was a hospital so I could sort myself out. It wasn't a bad place. It's not at all how the movies or television depict it to be. It's not a so-called "looney bin" for "head cases." It's just a place for helping and healing.

I snapped out of my trance and flicked my cigarette out of the window. I got lost in the past again. Sometimes I couldn't help it. The past would just crawl back in and sneak up on me. I started my little car, shifted, and pulled out of the Open House Bar and Grill's parking lot. My usual coffee sounded good, and I was ready to go home and relax.

5

"Dad, I'm home," I yelled as I walked into the little two-bedroom apartment.

There was a decent sized flat-screen television on the wall, a couch in the middle of the room, some family photos on the wall, two small coffee tables, and a rug. It wasn't much, but I did the best I could for us.

"Dad, you in your room?" I shouted out.

"Yeah, I'm in here," he responded.

I was surprised to find him lying in his bed. He would usually be in the living room watching terrible day-time television. His oxygen tank was propped up next to him, although he wasn't wearing the face mask.

My dad was diagnosed with chronic obstructive pulmonary disease some years ago after he was retired, and, after my mother had passed from cancer, I didn't want him living alone; plus, the hospital bills from my mother's visits and chemotherapy added up on him fast and he found himself in debt very quickly. I had no choice but to move him in with me, and I believed he liked the company. I didn't mind either. I was close to my father. I always regarded him as a great man, although he was a car mechanic and led a normal blue-collar existence all his life. But he was my hero when I was a boy and was good company as an adult.

"What's up?" I asked. "How come you aren't out there?"

"Oh, I was a little tired, so I decided to lay down for a bit."

He was getting older, and I didn't blame him for wanting to rest. I was just concerned. My dad was all that I had left besides my brother, Marcus, who I hadn't seen since mom passed. We were all heartbroken after my mother, especially my father. My mom was the love of his life, and he never thought that he would lose her so soon or thought that she would end up leaving that way. He was tired. I felt for him, even though I had my own pain to deal with.

"Did you eat?" I asked him.

"A little for lunch, but nothing that really filled me up."

"Okay. I'll get us something for dinner in a bit."

I put a hand on his chest, smiled, and then left the room.

In my room, I was sitting on my bed with my acoustic guitar and gently strumming chords while looking around. I was in a daze again, playing guitar on autopilot. I wondered how much more time I had with my father. Would he leave this world in pain like my mother? Do I have five more years with him or ten? I was often hard on myself. My conscience mind ridiculed me often, and it grew easier to argue silently within my own self. As someone with schizophrenia, I found it confusing when I was at odds. My mind would often go to dark places, corners that seemed bleak inside my head. I didn't enjoy it. I would sometimes try to think how I was before I was diagnosed. How did my mind work then? But I was very young at eighteen years old and nineteen. I was thirty-five, and those two worlds were miles apart. I just did my best to maintain my sanity each day and live a normal life. The medicines I was prescribed helped. I was on five different medications, and I only knew what one of them did to me. But it was okay. I understood that I was part patient, and part guinea pig in the psychology field. I was a specimen. I didn't mind if I wasn't hearing voices and wasn't confused on what was reality. I preferred normality.   I   lust   for   it.

2

<u>Chapter 2</u>

1

The next morning at work, I was portioning pickles in bags to six ounces for our fried pickle appetizer.

"How was last night?" Terry asked. "Did you do anything?"

"No," I said. "Just stayed in."

"Sounds boring."

"It was. I do not live an exciting life like you."

He laughed. "We cannot all be me. No matter how hard you all try."

"Sam?" I heard a voice call out. It was Vanessa the front-of-house manager. I stopped what I was doing and looked over at her.

An attractive woman who looked to be in her late twenties appeared in the kitchen window with Vanessa.

"Sam," my manager said, "This is Jen. She's our new waitress.

My gloved hands were covered in pickle juice, so I refrained from the usual handshake, and I opted to I wave and say "hi" instead.

"Nice to meet you," Jen said.

She was very cute, and I felt myself get nervous. I became tense. I hadn't felt this in a very long time. Something about her shook my nerves. Maybe it was the way her hair lay on the side of her face, or her almond shaped eyes—I wasn't sure.

For the next few hours, I could not get Jen, the new girl, out of my head. Her appearance was very attractive to me. I watched her through the window every time she came to grab her plates. She smiled softly. She would look up at us through the kitchen window and her eyes had a certain glow. I found myself captivated by her essence. So much so that I almost burnt my hand during the lunch rush because I was so distracted. She was short, blond, and had nice curves. She seemed sweet, and I liked that.

2

After the rush, Greg asked me to make patties, which for me was a daily routine. I knew we would need them prepped for the day. I grabbed my large stainless-steel bowl.

"She's cute," Terry said.

I grabbed myself a couple of latex gloves.

"Yeah," I replied. I didn't want him to know that I was instantly attracted to Jen. I'm sure Terry would have his jokes, no matter if he could tell I liked her or not.

I needed to go get two large tubes of hamburger meat.

"I know she gave *me* a boner." He laughed.

I continued my hamburger patties.

By the time the late afternoon rolled around, and it was time for all of us to clock out and go into the world once again, I had done all my tasks for the day and some. I was tired and ready to go. But before I went home, I stopped by the café for a pick me up from the day so that I may be inspired to write music tonight. Although we hadn't practiced in weeks, I still enjoyed writings songs and rehearsing the old material in my bedroom.

As Greg left the restaurant, he extended a hand into the air, "Have a good day, guys. I'm out."

Terry followed, and I was next out the door. I made my way to my small car. After getting in. I lit a cigarette. Sat there for a moment, let the car idle, and then put it into gear.

She was on my mind—I couldn't shake the feeling or

sensation—Jen was under my skin like a splinter. It was her allure. Those green eyes—were her eyes *green?* I had forgotten. It had been a few hours. I had made certain not to interact too much with her for the rest of the shift. Maybe they were just blue. Anyhow, she was someone I wanted to get to know, but I didn't want to be obvious about it. The last thing I wanted was to be the butt of anyone's jokes, whether it was Terry or someone else making them. I didn't enjoy being made fun of.

I pulled into the café's parking lot, found a space, and hopped out. Even though it was late in the year, it was hot outside. Texas is always hot—I didn't enjoy that fact about the state where I lived much, but it made the cool fronts especially nice and remarkable when they *did* blow in.

"What can I get started for you today?" the barista asked, after I approached the counter.

I told her I only wanted a regular coffee with cream and lots of sugar.

"Name?"

"Sam," I said.

I loved the aroma of this place. It reminded me of when I was a boy, and my mom would make breakfast on weekends. Our house would be filled with the smell of eggs, bacon, and, of course, rich coffee with a hint of cinnamon. As a child, I would watch Saturday morning cartoons while my dad looked at his hotrod magazines, and mother would make breakfast. It was pleasant. I had a wonderful childhood.

After I finished ordering, I stepped to the side and leaned against a table to wait for my coffee to arrive. It was about the small things in life, and this was certainly one of those little treats I could give myself after a long, hard day at work. I could not afford much. I was taking care of myself and my father. The instruments I did have, and equipment, I bought before my mother died. Everything was from years ago.

As I waited, I could smell all the spices in the shop. Cinnamon, like when I was a child, and nutmeg. It was a small place, so the aroma filled it up quickly and it was very robust to the nostrils. I realized how loud the coffee shop was. There were a few tables in the middle of the shop, and people sat and talked in pairs or tables of three. Some people had their noses buried in books and in their laptop computers, while a boy with his father stood waiting by the wall for their order. There was an older woman by the bathroom door, and finally a woman about my age with a pen and spiral. She looked to be writing a lengthy prose on paper.

I wonder what she's conspiring.

She had vibrant red hair with blond streaks throughout, jewelry all over her neck and fingers, and a quirky grin. I supposed she amused herself with her own writings. I felt like I was intruding just by staring, so I looked away after a moment.

"Sam!" the barista yelled out.

That was me!

3

Later that evening, after I was home and checked on dad, I retired to my room. I kicked off my non-slip shoes, laid on the bed, and took out a book to help me relax. It was a long day, and I was curious how the next chapter in the book I was reading would go.

I must have dozed off because I woke up on top of the blankets with the book on my chest and the light on. I picked up my phone and it read 2:35 a.m. Shit. I got out of bed and made my way into the living room. Dad had fallen asleep too, but to evening television. He was propped up on the sofa with his eyes closed and oxygen mask on. I didn't want to disturb him. He looked peaceful. I turned back, hit the lights in my room, and crawled into bed.

The next day at work, I did everything to avoid the new waitress, Jen. When I wasn't on the fryers, I was out getting the dish cart and washing everything after the lunch rush. I stayed with my head low and kept my concentration on work, although I very much wanted to start up a conversation. I wanted to know her story.

I had both my hands in the dish pit when Terry walked over.

"It's a little obvious what you're doing," he said.

I stopped and looked at him.

"She can probably tell you like her. It's clear you're avoiding her. I think she even asked you when her chicken tenders were up, and you didn't say two words to her. Why don't you just go talk to her? Say something, man. I'm having a hard time watching you squirm in here." He laughed. "You know those puppies that run out into the road and get hit because no one was watching them and then they come back up to their owner's yard all limping and crying and shit? Well, that's you, Sam, and I can't just stand here and watch it happen."

Jen must have come to the back of the kitchen where we were because Terry looked over my shoulder.

"Yo, new girl," he said while waiving her over to us.

"God, Terry. Shut the fuck up!" I dropped the pan I was scrubbing and scrambled to dry my hands.

"New girl," he said again as she approached with a smile. "My buddy here is wondering your name."

I lowered my head. I wanted to drown myself in the sink.

"Oh," she said. "I thought I told it to you guys already. I'm Jen."

I turned around and stood still next to Terry.

Before I could get him to shut his mouth, he kept on. "Sam likes you. He says you're pretty. Prettier than the other waitresses."

I wanted to die. All I could get out was, "I didn't tell him that. Terry is confused. I don't think you're pretty."

She looked offended.

"I mean—," I was drowning in my own words. "— you are pretty. Hot."

"Um, okay?"

She didn't seem impressed by me or my whimpering puppy dog charm.

"Let me help out my friend here, Jen," Terry interjected. "He wants to go out and have a drink with you. He might even buy you dinner. What do you say?"

I was red and feeling hot all over. At this point, all I wanted to do was clock out and leave this embarrassment.

"Yes," she replied to Terry, "I'll go out with him."

She looked redder than me, but she obliged to Terry's antics. I was amazed. He had pulled it off! He had done the impossible and got me a date with the beautiful new waitress who had been haunting me since she started.

"When should he pick you up?" my cocky, yet astonishing and gifted friend asked.

Jen replied, "I'll give him my number here in a bit after I clean the dining room." She looked up at me. "I'm excited. I can't wait."

13

She walked to the front of the restaurant.

I turned to Terry and punched him in the arm. "How the fuck did you do that?"

"I'm a smooth operator," he replied to me with a devil's grin. "I have that magic touch, I suppose."

Greg came out of the kitchen. "Terry, if you're done playing matchmaker now, I need you in here ASAP!"

"Shit. Gotta go!"

3

Chapter 3

1

The rest of the afternoon I was scared and shaking in my non-slip shoes. I was fumbling when completing ticket orders and doing dishes. I was happy though, too. I smiled a little more than usual and I felt bright inside.

I couldn't believe I was going to go on a date with Jen. I could have jumped. But I tried to remain cool and casual as I continued my work for the rest of the day. We ran into each other, Jen and I, a few times. We said little, but we both knew what was to happen.

Later, when it was time to clock out, I went up to her and asked if I could have her number.

"Sure," she said. "When's our date?"

"I hadn't thought of that yet, but I'll let you know tonight, if that's okay?"

She smiled. "Cool."

I turned away from her, put in my code into the computer to clock out, and left the Open House Bar and Grill a changed man. It had been some time since I had been on a date. I was ready.

After I got into my little, beat-up coupe and drove away from the lot of the restaurant, I headed to the café to get my usual coffee. Jen was on my mind as I was driving. I thought of her long blond hair and gorgeous eyes. I couldn't help myself but fantasize about what our date might be like—if I could gather myself to choose a place and time and keep my schizophrenic brain under control.

I pulled into the café's parking lot still thinking of Jen when I slammed into something. My car came to a halt. I was shaken, but I assumed I was okay. I was caught in a daydream and had hit something— no, someone! I got out of my car before I could think of myself. I had run into someone else's car.

"Shit!" the woman exclaimed, while exiting her vehicle. Her hands on her head, eyes full of tears— she was aggravated.

"I'm so sorry," I said, as I came around my little coupe only to witness my front-end had collided with her rear bumper.

"Did you not see me?" she asked. "Did you not see me backing out?"

I—I didn't know." It was all I could get out.

"Right," she continued. "You just *had* to run into me. It's just my fucking luck; just the thing I needed to finish off my day."

She was the same woman I had seen sitting and jotting down notes in the shop— the woman that stuck out like a rose in a sunflower field. She had red hair and a soft face. But right now, she was furious, and her cheeks were red—her eyes were swollen with angry tears.

I was a ghost, pale and dead. I didn't know what to tell her. She was furious.

"I have insurance," I said. "I can get my information for you."

"Yes," she replied. "I'll need it. It was clearly *your* fault."

I agreed. I went back to my car and reached into the glove compartment. I stepped back out with my insurance in hand, and we exchanged information.

"Should we exchange numbers?" I asked her.

"Yes. Let me grab a pen." She opened her door and took out a pen with a scrap piece of paper from the center console of her dented SUV. "What is it?"

I gave her my number, and after a moment of looking over her bumper and taking a couple of photos, she got back into her SUV. I got into my little sedan and backed away so she could pull out. I waved as she took off, but she didn't return the gesture. Although I had just been in a minor fender bender, I got my coffee like I always had.

I knew she was upset and angry, but I couldn't afford the hassle either. It's not like I wanted to run into her giant SUV. I was reluctant to call my insurance when I got home. I didn't want to have to pay for her new bumper or any damages that I may have caused. I couldn't afford it right now, especially taking care of my father. But one thing I did have to spruce up my mood was Jen's number, and no fender bender accident could take that away from me. So, I sipped on my usual coffee as I drove home.

2

After I pulled into the apartment complex, I had an idea of where I might take Jen. I was thinking of a steak house this coming weekend if she agreed. I was rusty at dating and had never really been too good at charming the opposite sex. I wasn't confident, I didn't know the *right* things to say, and— I certainly wasn't the most *handsome* guy out there. But she must have said *yes* for a reason, and that thought alone made me pull out my phone and call her up.

"Hello?" Jen answered after a few rings.

"Hey. It's Sam from work. I was calling about our date. I was thinking this weekend— Saturday— we could go to Charlie's Steakhouse. Seven o'clock work for you?"

"Yeah!"

She didn't hesitate and that reassured me that maybe going out with the pretty waitress would be less stressful than I had thought. We talked for another minute or two then said bye. I put the cell phone back in my pocket and got out of my car. I had forgotten about the mishap at the coffee shop until I looked at the passenger seat with the insurance laying on top. The scrap paper with the woman's name and number lay next to it on the seat.

What was her name anyway?

I grabbed the paper and read it. "Cecilia," it read, written in blue pen. Underneath was her number.

I stuffed the number in the pocket of my jeans and headed up to my apartment on the second floor.

"Dad?" I called out as I stepped inside.

I didn't see him on the couch, and this worried me. I dropped

17

my keys on the table that stood next to the door and ran into his room.

"Dad!"

He was on the floor lying face down. I ran to him and crouched down to turn him over.

"Are you alright? What happened?"

He came to as I turned him over in my arms.

"Where am I? I think I fell."

My dad wasn't wearing his oxygen mask and maybe he had gotten winded when he was going for his afternoon nap. He must have passed out before he could reach the bed.

"I forgot my oxygen in the living room," he said, as he lay still in my arms. "I'm okay. I guess. I just fell."

"You can't be moving around too much without wearing your face mask," I told him.

"I know, I know," he said, as I helped him up to his feet, then onto the edge of the bed. "I wish I had one of those *sexy* live-in nurses."

"You know I can't afford that," I replied with a smile.

"If only," my dad said. He chuckled.

"Don't do that again," I said. "Scared me half to death."

"I didn't mean to. I scared *myself*."

We laughed.

"Bring beer?" my dad asked me.

"You know you can't drink either."

"Worth a shot."

I sat next to him on the edge of the bed with an arm around his shoulder. He was getting older. My boyhood hero was aging faster than I wanted, and that thought scared me— as did losing him one day. Hopefully not *too* soon.

"I love you, Dad," I said to him.

I didn't mean to stare at him, but my dad meant the world to me. I loved him very much.

"I love you too, Sam," he replied.

We looked at each other for a moment.

Then he laughed and said, "You can leave now."

I got up and left my dad's room.

I made my way to the kitchen to scrounge up ideas for the night's dinner when I felt my phone go off. I looked down and it was

Jen.

"*Hi.*"

I replied to the text, "*Hey there.*"

I was dull. I didn't know how to respond. I wasn't a *stud* like some others out there in the world; I lacked confidence in myself to deliver what I really thought and wanted to say. I didn't know how to get myself across to females.

"*I forgot to mention,*" she said, "*that I'm off tomorrow so I won't see you until the date.*"

"Oh, okay," I replied. "*Well, I very much look forward to it.*"

I was an idiot. I didn't know how to elaborate my true thoughts. The texting was killing me. I was sure I was better in person.

"*I'll see you then,*" she finished. I put my phone away.

I looked around in the fridge for something to cook for my dad and me. There wasn't much. I wasn't very good at stocking up the kitchen. When I wasn't home, dad survived on coffee and chocolate cookies.

I went back into his room to ask him if he wanted hamburgers or chicken breasts for dinner, but I found him asleep, tidy in his bed. He looked comfortable and I didn't want to disturb him, especially after the little spill he had earlier. I closed the door and left the apartment to go find myself a burger somewhere. For the rest of the night, Jen, and even Cecilia, were on my mind.

4

Chapter 4

1

It was Saturday evening, and I was getting ready for the date with Jen. I put on my best shirt and jeans, cleaned off my tennis shoes, and found some decent smelling cologne. I was looking for a brush when I stumbled upon Cecilia's phone number on my nightstand. Although our meeting was the result of me running into her SUV, I liked her. She was this strange, pretty girl that sit in my coffee shop on a hot and humid afternoon in South Texas. I admired her from afar. Even though we had finally met, I would have never imagined her to be so irate about something as little as a dented bumper. But it was my fault. I was to blame. It was up to me to pay for the damages.

I came back to reality and pushed Cecilia's number away from me.

I have to hurry up. I was going to be late.

It was almost six-thirty when I left the apartment. I hurried down to my little car. Jen wanted to meet instead of me picking her up, which I was fine with. My car wasn't that impressive. So, I made my way through the city to Charlie's Steakhouse.

As I drove and the sun set, I thought about my father. I hoped he would be alright. His health was increasingly declining over the past few years, and I was very concerned. He was due for a doctor's appointment. But they always told us the same things—keep him on oxygen, make sure he takes his prescribed medication, stay active—there were never any changes to the doc's orders. I wanted my dad to be okay. As I grew older, he became older too. And closer to being gone.

I tried not to think about my father so much as I pulled into the lot of Charlie's Steakhouse. I found a spot and hopped out of my little coupe. I pulled out my phone.

"*I'm here.*" Jen had sent a text ten minutes earlier.

I made my way to the entrance.

"How many?" the hostess asked me as I got through the door.

"I'm meeting someone," I replied.

"Okay," she said, and waved me in.

I went around the hostess's booth and looked around for Jen. I found her after a moment. She looked stunning in a black dress with silver earrings. I could tell she put on makeup. She stood up and greeted me with a smile and then a soft hug. She smelt terrific. I hoped my cologne wasn't overbearing.

"I wasn't sure if you were going to make it," she said, teasing.

"Oh, yeah. I wouldn't miss this for *anything.*"

"Did you find parking okay?" She looked deep into my eyes across from across the table with a smile. She messed with the ends of her hair, wrapping them in her fingers.

I was in a trance. From the get-go she had me hooked.

"Yes," I replied. "Parking was fine."

A waiter walked over to the table.

He asked, "Can I start you two off with something to drink?"

Jen looked at me. I suppose she was unsure if we were *drinking* or just sipping soft drinks.

"I'll have a beer," I replied.

"Rum and coke," she added with a grin.

"I'll be right back with your drinks," the waiter said and withdrew from the table.

"Have you ever been here before?" Jen asked me.

She kept smiling at me. I liked it.

"Once or twice—with my dad, but that was years ago." I didn't want to say too much. I didn't want her to think I was some idiot that spoke too much of himself; I also didn't want to say too little either. In the back of my mind, I was searching for the perfect balance for our conversation. I just didn't want to be an *idiot.*

"Awesome," she replied. "I've never been here. I'm surprised I wasn't the late one. I don't live anywhere near this part of town actually."

Great. I had picked a terrible restaurant for our first date. I am *an* idiot.

"Oh? Where do you live?" I asked her. I was trying to keep the conversation alive. I didn't want to bore her. The last thing I wanted was for her to cut the date short. I would have to live with that at work. I guess that's why they say, "Don't shit where you eat."

She was looking around. I wondered if she was nervous too because she appeared to be impatiently waiting for her drink, searching for it, anticipating its arrival. Her eyes were wandering around the restaurant until our drinks came to the table and the waiter asked if we were ready to order.

"Yes," I said loudly, trying to cut through the chatter of the dinner crowd that filled up Charlie's. I had my menu up. I could only see Jen's eyes over her menu, too. "You go first," I told her.

"Okay." She looked up at the waiter. "I'll have the ten ounce sirloin— "

Jesus! She's going to be expensive.

"—medium-rare, with mashed potatoes, loaded." She looked at the waiter to make sure he was writing all her over-priced order down on his little notepad. "With the asparagus."

I almost dropped my menu, along with my jaw.

What in the world? Does she think I was made of money? Or had I just not been on a proper date in ages? Can't wait for the check.

"Yeah," I said, grabbing the waiter's attention, "I'll have the hamburger steak with mushrooms and onions, green beans, and a potato." I put my menu on the table and looked at Jen. "Plain," I added, looking at her, but addressing the waiter.

She had run up the bill, I was sure. I would be paying for this dinner for the next decade. Not to mention that run-in with the red-haired girl at the coffee shop. I had to pay for that too! And my dad's upcoming doctor's appointment. I was stressed even more now.

We continued our evening over small chit-chat as we waited for her twenty-five-dollar-steak to arrive along with my plate that I'm sure was under fifteen dollars—and that was with the beer.

"How long have you been at the Open House restaurant?" Jen asked me, then took a sip of her rum and coke.

"Good question," I replied. "I've been there off and on for about ten years. I've tried other jobs, but the kitchen always calls me back in some way or another. I just kind of *fell* into cooking; I'm good at it. I don't know. It's what I do best, I suppose. Have you always been a waitress?"

"Yeah," Jen replied. "I've been a waitress on and off since I was able to work at sixteen. *I'm good at it.* Kind of like you, restaurants have always been a constant in my life." She smirked.

Our food arrived after about twenty minutes or so, and she appeared happy. I was happy too. She was everything I had fantasized about, and I was ecstatic to share the night with her. I couldn't imagine an evening more pleasant than with Jen at Charlie's Steakhouse. I was content in this moment. Even the hamburger steak was good.

2

After about an hour and a half at the table together, we figured it was time to get up and go. I walked in front of her, leading the way to the exit. I wasn't sure if I was to hold her hand and guide her through the crowd.

Maybe that's second date material?

I turned and made sure she was following. At my relief, she was close behind with a quaint smile looking back up at me. If I would have died in this moment, I would have been content and happy.

We made our way through the crowd and out the double doors.

She turned to me. "Are you working tomorrow?" she asked.

I thought for a moment and said, "I believe so. Are you?"

"Yes," she said with a smile.

I couldn't get over how cute she looked in that dress—it was almost *sexy*—and I hadn't seen her like this.

"I'm going to grab my jacket from the car," she told me. She walked away and I strolled over to a wooden bench that was near the entrance of Charlie's.

I guess we were going to continue our date for a while longer.

I was thrilled to see her come back with a large red coat.

"It's my favorite," she said, as she swung it around and put it on. "My mother gave it to me last year as a Christmas gift."

"Very cool," I replied. "Wait," I then said to her. I was reminded of my father. I took out my cellphone and looked to make sure he hadn't sent a text while we were at dinner. "Sorry. It's just my dad. Just making sure he's okay."

"Do you need to call him?" She appeared concerned, which I appreciated.

"No, no—he'll be okay. He's at home, but I do check my phone in case of emergencies. You never know. He had a spill recently."

"Is he okay?" she asked. She sat down on the wooden bench. It was faded. The wood slightly rotted, but still a quaint place to sit beneath the night sky.

"Yes. But it did scare me a little," I replied.

"What happened?"

Her eyes were like two moons next to one another in a night sky that an alien culture in some galaxy far away might worship—or maybe by the ancient cultures of this planet before they knew Christianity and God. Her gaze hypnotized me and I stumbled over what I wanted to say.

"I'm sorry," she said. "I'm imposing. It's none of my business. I don't know *you* and I don't know your *dad.*"

"You're fine. He lost his breath—oxygen—he has a tank that he has to wear most of the time. Maybe you'll meet him one day. He's a sweet guy. Very nice."

Jen smiled. "I'd like that."

As she looked down into her folded hands, I noticed a bit of sadness looming over her.

"Are you okay?" I asked.

"Yeah," she responded rather quickly. "What do you want to do now?"

"I mean—"

"It's still early," she said then laughed. "Don't be a bore! We'll keep the night going."

"Ummm …" I was at a loss for words and all I could get out

24

was, "How about another drink?"

She appeared to think about my question.

Did she really want to continue the night some more with me?

She had a devil's grin with a spice in her eyes alongside a fiery twinkle that shimmered from the iris. "Okay," she said. "Let's do it!"

"Follow me," I said.

She got up and as I got into my car, she got into hers. I pulled out of the parking space and headed out the lot. I drove west to a small tavern that I knew of about ten or so minutes away from Charlie's.

Hope she's enjoying the date. I hope I'm not too dull or lacking charm. If she didn't like me—why bother? She wouldn't be hanging out after our dinner.

It was dark out when we got there. The only light was from street lamps and the neon sign above the door that read, "Shirley's Place."

"I've never been here," Jen said. "I don't think I've even heard of it."

"It's a little dive. A small place. But they have great drink specials, and the beer isn't too pricey," I replied, as I grabbed for the door's long vertical handle.

The door groaned as I opened it and waved Jen inside. I followed close behind. Inside, it was dark and musty. It had a lingering smell of incense and old beer.

Maybe it was a better bar a few years ago.

The bartender was a young guy—maybe twenty-seven—but he was casual and had a big smile.

"Welcome to Shirley's!" he said. "What can I get you two?"

I looked down at Jen and she looked up at me.

"Whatever you want," I told her. "It's on me."

I had already paid for dinner, but I didn't mind paying more here. It was a date, and I hadn't been on a date in a few years. I hope she couldn't tell I was nervous and excited by the shaking of my hands. I stumbled over my words occasionally too. My mouth would become dry. I hope I wasn't too transparent.

Jen told the bartender, "I guess I'll just take a Bud."

The young man looked over at me next.

"Yes, for me as well," I shouted over the music.

In a moment, he set two long-neck beers on the wooden bar.

The bottle was cold and frosty when I gripped its neck. I took a quick sip, then gestured for Jen to follow me. We made our way to a table and we both sat.

"Thanks for inviting me out," she said.

"Well, actually, it was Terry who asked." I laughed. "Don't get me wrong—you are beautiful— but I just don't think I would have gotten the courage to ask you on a date like this without him."

"I see," she replied. She looked down at her beer and then back to me. She stared into my eyes and said, "I'm glad he did though. I'm really enjoying the night."

I smiled, then took a sip, then looked away. I was a little embarrassed. I wasn't confident and I didn't think she liked me, but I guess I was wrong.

As we were sitting there drinking our beers, Michael Jackson's "Beat It" came on the jukebox.

"Oh my God, I love this song," Jen said, leaning in towards me and on the edge of her seat on the small table.

"Yeah, he's great," I replied, although Michael Jackson was not one of my favorites. He may have been a huge Pop star, but just not my taste.

She started to shake her shoulders and lip-sync the song. She put the beer to her lips and pretended it was a microphone.

"Beat it! Beat it!" she sang aloud.

I smiled and stared. She was amazing and more than I could have hoped for.

After an hour, we left Shirley's Place and staggered out the door together holding hands.

"You were great in there," I said, laughing. She hadn't just sung "Beat it", but a few others as the night went on. "A regular karaoke master."

"Thank you. Thank you."

We made our way to her car and stood outside of it. I looked down at her and stared into her eyes. I felt like she wanted me to lean in and kiss her, but I refrained.

"Well, good night," I said, then turned and walked to my car. I didn't look back out of fear. I didn't want rejection. I didn't want it so soon as I had had a great time as well with the new waitress from the Open House Bar and Grill.

What an idiot. Loser, why didn't you go in for the kiss?

I got into my little tin can of a car and started the engine. I would go home and call it a night. But it was an amazing time that I will never forget.

3

The next day at work, Jen wasn't there, and that was kind of a relief. I guess she didn't work like she had mentioned. I heard she wasn't feeling well. Honestly, I didn't want everyone else to know she and I went out together—at least not yet. I wasn't embarrassed by any means, but I didn't know how my coworkers would react to the news. I didn't want all the heckling.

As I was washing the dishes in the pit, Terry walked up beside me.

"How did it go, Sam?" he asked.

I kept silent.

"Not good? Eh, that's okay," he said, "She was too pretty for you anyhow." He laughed.

I put down the plate and looked at him irritated. I knew he would be one of the first to give me a hard time. "It was fine," I said with a stern voice. "We had fun."

"Did you get the ol' willy wet?"

Terry pushed my shoulder.

"She's a sweet girl," I replied. "We didn't do anything like that—had some dinner, had a drink and that was it."

"I bet," Terry snickered.

He left fortunately. I continued the dishes.

Although I had a good time out last night with Jen, I kept thinking of the red-haired woman from the coffee shop. Cecilia was a mystery to me and intrigued me.

Now she *was something else.*

She had curves, gorgeous eyes, and even though she wasn't too happy about her bumper, she had a nice smile. If I could choose, Cecilia would be my next date.

Maybe I can text her or give the mystery woman a call? No, that's silly—she wouldn't even give me the time of day, unless I was paying for the damages on her car. Why risk humility? Don't put yourself in that situation only to be embarrassed. She would shut you down immediately. Don't do it!

"Hey!" Greg hollered from the kitchen. "Sam, can you come here? I need your help on the line."

I put the dish down, rinsed off my arms and hands, and headed for   the   line.

5

Chapter 5

1

It was two-thirty, and I was taking a break outside smoking a cigarette. I peered around. The air was humid without a breeze, and all was calm around me. The trees didn't move, the debris on the ground was still, and I admired all the previous cigarette butts I had tossed on the ground over so many days of working at the restaurant.

My pocket buzzed and I took out my cellphone.

"Don't forget about my appointment at three," Dad wrote to me via text.

Shit.

He told me about his doctor's appointment last week, but it had slipped my mind. I threw my cigarette and went back into the kitchen.

I walked up to Greg. "Hey. Do you mind if I take off early? My dad's got to go to the doctor at three o'clock," I told him.

"Just finish up the dish cart and you can go, Sam."

Greg was a nice guy. He had run the kitchen since it had opened years ago. He had stuck with the owner through thick and thin and was valuable to the Open House Bar and Grill.

I hurried and finished off the cart, clocked out, then high-tailed it to my car. I started the engine and put a cigarette in my mouth. After lighting it, I pulled out of the lot. I was about ten minutes from our apartment complex. I didn't want dad to be too late. He moved slow at sixty-years-old though and we were on the second floor. We would have to hurry to see the doctor at a decent time.

After a bit of driving, I pulled into the complex and found a space to park in. I hopped out, ran up the stairs of our building, and burst through the door.

"Dad, are you ready?" I yelled out into the apartment.

"In here," he replied.

I walked into his room and he was putting on his shoes.

"Dad, where's your socks?"

"Son, at my age, it's impossible to get those damn things on. I'm fine. Let's go!"

I helped him up off the bed. He walked beside me and next to him he rolled the oxygen tank.

"We're going to be late, Sam," he said to me, as we made our way out of the front door.

I turned and locked up without a word.

"You were supposed to be here a long time ago," he continued.

"Dad, I know, but I got caught up at work. If we hurry, we can get to the doctor's soon and I'm sure Dr. Ferguson will still see you."

"Point is, Sam— "

We waddled down the stairs with the oxygen tank beside my father.

"— point is that you need to be on time for appointments. We're not going to be there at three o'clock, and now I'm going to look like an *idiot*."

"You're not going to look like an idiot, Dad. The doctor will understand."

My father was very anal about being on time to places, appointments, and events. He had always been that way. Even when I was a boy, he was like that.

"Your mother wouldn't have been late," my dad said, as we made our way into the lot and to the car.

"I know, Dad. But mom was a housewife too and didn't have a full-time job like I do," I replied. I opened the passenger door and eased my father and his tank inside. It fit nicely between his legs and into his lap.

"Your mother would have been home at two o'clock!" My dad kept on me as I shut the door and made my way to the driver's side.

I got in.

"Are you buckled?" I asked him. He looked over with his mask off. I picked it up off his chin and placed it over his mouth. I then put on his seat belt and fastened it tight. "Hold on! If we're going to make it at a decent time, I'll have to rush." I backed out as quickly as I could from the parking space and put my little Toyota in gear. After a moment, we headed down the street.

I heard my father's loud inhaling. I wanted to turn the radio on, but I didn't want to be rude. He didn't deserve to be ignored.

"Son, " he said, "Thank you."

He put his hand on top of my hand as we made our way to the doctor's office across town.

"For what, dad?" I asked him.

"After your mother died …" he coughed into his mask, "I felt very alone. You didn't have to move me in with you. I appreciate that. I always will."

"Thanks, dad."

I could tell he was genuine. But I was concerned.

Why was he speaking this way? Was he okay?

Finally, we reached the offices in Square Plaza. I parked and hurried around the car to get my dad out and inside the building. He stumbled over himself, but I managed to get him out unscathed.

"Let's go, son!"

Even though we were pressed for time, I was enjoying this outing with my father. It was very seldom he left the apartment.

I grabbed the door for him, and he entered with a slow stroll.

"Hey, Mary!" My dad smiled at the front desk lady and all of her coworkers. "How have you all been?"

"You'll need to sign in," she replied. "But we're all doing well, Mr. Williams."

My dad picked up the clipboard that the woman passed through the slot on the bottom of the window. He followed me close behind as we found a couple of very uncomfortable chairs in the waiting room.

"What's my name again?" My dad looked at me with a grin.

"Dad, hurry," I replied. "You want to be seen today. Right?"

"Yes," he said, as he took up the pen and began filling the form out. It took him a few minutes, but after he was finished, I took it out of his grip and returned it to the front desk.

"The doctor will see your father shortly," the woman said to me. I nodded and took my seat again.

"I think they're just drawing some blood today, Sam. I'm pretty sure it's just a check-up. I don't think they'll do much if you just want to wait out here."

I was fine with waiting. I didn't mind it. Even if it took an hour or so for the appointment, I was patient. One thing my dad instilled in me when I was young was *patience*.

We sat there for about fifteen minutes. My dad had knocked out and I thought he was drooling, in fact. Then a young woman came out from behind the door that led to the offices.

"Mr. Williams," she called out.

My dad, startled, woke up from his nap.

Maybe he was dreaming of mom?

"Here. I'm here," he said, shaken up. He rose to his feet slowly, grabbed his oxygen tank, and made his way to the young woman. They disappeared to the back together after a moment at the door.

My phone went off in my pocket. I had a message. I reached in and took it out. It read Jen's name on the screen in the notifications box. I unlocked my phone and opened the message.

"*Hey, you,*" she said.

I sat there, thinking of something clever to write. After a while, I had nothing and wrote, "*Hey.*" I waited a few moments. Then, the phone went off again in my hand.

She wrote, "*I haven't gotten to see you since our date, and I just wanted to tell you that I had a great time with you. I'm happy you asked me out!*"

I smiled and closed my phone. I wasn't sure how to reply so I refrained from a quick response. I was content now that somebody out in the world liked me. She was pretty and I guess I hadn't bored her to death.

Good going, Sam. You're a winner.

2

"So, what did the doctor say?" I asked my dad, as we headed back to the apartment.

"Same old, same old, Sam. He never has anything new to say. Always the same *bull*. Which reminds me, when is *your* appointment for your psychiatrist visit?"

I saw a psych doctor once a month towards the end of the month. He would prescribe my meds and talk to me somewhat. If everything was going okay at home and work, my doctor really didn't say much or give me any advice whatsoever.

"In a week or two, I believe, Dad."

We were about five minutes away from the apartment. I wanted to stop by the coffee shop and grab a drink before we got home.

"Do I get one too?" my father asked me, as I pulled into the shop's parking lot.

"Do you want a coffee?" I asked him with a smile.

"I'm just kidding, Sam. Go and get your coffee."

I got out, shut my door, and headed inside the coffee shop. As I went in, I saw Cecilia sitting in the corner of the shop alone reading. I don't think she saw me when I entered, which was a relief. I hoped she wouldn't get up and approach me. I couldn't bear the shame. I went to the counter and ordered my usual. I looked around some more and stared at her over my shoulder. She was gorgeous. A woman more than a man such as I could ever hope to ask out. She looked up and I turned away. I stared at the barista's computer. I hoped Cecilia hadn't noticed me standing there waiting for my coffee. Finally, it was ready. So, I picked it up off the counter and bolted out the door.

"Everything okay?" my father asked me, as I got into my little Toyota car.

"Yeah, yeah," I replied. We left the shop's parking lot and headed for the apartment.

As we drove in silence, I thought about Cecilia and all the mysteries that surrounded her. I only knew that she wrote in a journal, and hated her bumper being bashed in by complete strangers. I pushed her out of my head as we pulled into the complex.

"Home," my dad sighed as I parked the car. "Do you mind helping me get out, Sam?"

"Of course," I told him, as I unbuckled my seatbelt. I went around the front of the car. Dad had already opened the door. I held it open and put out my arm for him to latch onto. His weight pulled me down a bit, but I was strong and could help him out of the car and onto his feet.

"After you," my dad said.

"Don't forget your tank."

"Right. Right," he said, as he turned back and lifted the tall oxygen tank out of the floorboard of the car.

We made our way up to the second story and got into the apartment unscathed.

"I guess we made it okay. Huh, Sam?" my dad said, as he headed for the couch.

"Yeah, dad."

He sat and turned on the television as I made my way down the hall and to my room. Inside, I kicked off my shoes. I sat on the edge of the bed and took a sip of my coffee. It wasn't so hot now that we were home.

I felt a little uncomfortable. I thought that maybe my anxiety was acting up from the doctor's visit. I reached over and grabbed a pill bottle off the nightstand. I took one and drank it with warm coffee. I didn't enjoy the times when I felt like my schizophrenia was too much for me. It wasn't every day—in fact, getting older, the symptoms have lessened: I didn't hear voices like when I was in my early twenties, I wasn't *as* paranoid as I used to be, and I only had a little anxiety to deal with. It could have been much worse. The doctor said I was a "high functioning" schizophrenic, which was fine with me if I wasn't hearing anything.

I used to imagine—when I was at my most delusional—that people were out to get me; I could hear them; but the strange thing about it was—looking back—that no one else knew or could hear what I had been hearing. It was hard. But with counseling and the right meds, over time, I became less paranoid.

The hospitals two years ago are where I started my monthly injections. The medicine worked. So, I didn't mind getting poked towards the end of each month. I wasn't cured, but I *damn right* felt it was a godsend.

I put my coffee down, laid on the full-sized bed, and took out my phone to check my messages. I wanted to see if Jen had sent me anything while I was driving from the doctor's office. No new text—it only read the last one from before. I placed my phone on my chest and looked over to the nightstand. Cecilia's number lay there wrinkled up. I had a strange urge to dial her up, but I refrained.

She didn't want to hear from me, unless it was about insurance. If only I was a little more handsome, or more confident—or if I had six-pack abs like some guys out there. Yeah, they get all the girls.

I closed my eyes and drifted off to sleep.

3

My phone was still on my chest. It woke me up when it went off. I looked at the screen and it was Jen.

She wrote, *"I'll see you in the morning."*

It was followed with a "smiling-face emoji." I grinned, then closed my eyes again.

4

The next morning, I woke up to see my father in the doorway of my room. He was holding a letter in his hand.

"What is it?" I asked him. I was confused. He stood there with the letter in his hand and his eyes were scrolling over it. "Is everything okay?"

"Son, they canceled my medical insurance."

I sat up on the edge of the bed. I was fully clothed. My hair disheveled.

"Says here something about the cost is going up, but my Social Security won't pay for it … I don't qualify anymore. 'We apologize, Mr. Williams.' It's all it says. What the *fuck?*"

"Don't worry, Dad. We'll figure it out."

"Son, if I don't have insurance, I can't get my prescriptions, I can't see the doctor—" He looked down at his oxygen tank. "They won't give me anymore of the *fucking things!*"

He knocked over the tank and flung the letter in the air. I didn't know what to do.

"Dad," I said, as I put my hands in the air, "calm down. I'll

35

figure out how to fix this."

"I'll die without this stupid tank, Samuel," my dad said, as he bent down to pick up the tank off its' side."

He started to calm down a little bit as I got up and put on my shoes.

"Don't worry," I told him. "I'll think it over at work." I put a hand on his shoulder then walked past him. "I've got to go. I'm running behind."

I left the apartment and headed for the Open House Bar and Grill for my shift.

5

As soon as I walked in, I saw Jen. She looked good today. She noticed me right away and smiled. I walked up to the machine to clock in and she was at the drink station making tea.

"How was your night?" she asked me, as I punched in my four-digit code.

I grabbed a cup to fill myself up with a drink from the fountain and replied, "It was fine. Same old, same old night in."

I wanted to keep it brief and maybe be *Mr. Cool*. I walked away to the back.

There, I was greeted by Terry.

"Hey, Sam," he said as I placed my drink down on the stainless-steel table. "Ready for another day, bitch?"

He was always so welcoming.

"See Jen?" he asked me with a grin followed by a snicker.

Terry was immature and got off on the gossip that circulated the Open House restaurant. I thought it was all childish and tried to stay out of it as much as I could.

"Yeah," I replied. "I did."

"Hit it yet?" he asked.

"No." I took a drink.

"Sam," Greg hollered from the grill, "Can you start bagging the calamari please?"

"On it!" I yelled back.

I left Terry on the expo line and made my way to the walk-in cooler. There was a box of calamari thawed out inside. I opened the box and took out two bags to take back to the kitchen. Six ounces was supposed to be the weight of each sandwich bag.

The lunch rush was the usual. I was at the fryer station helping Greg get the orders out. He would make the burger, I would place fries into a small basket, and then I would hand this dish to Terry to finish off with toppings and two slices of bacon—customer's choice of cheese, of course. For the chicken wings, Greg would drop six pieces, twelve pieces, or eighteen pieces into the right fryer. We had two fryers: the left and the right one. The left was primarily for fries. If I had to, and ran out of space in the *right,* I would drop my chicken fried steaks in the left fryer and fried appetizers—such as mozzarella sticks or fried mushrooms.

The usual eleven o'clock to one o'clock rush had come and gone. All of us in the back went up front and sat at a table near the kitchen entrance. We sat and looked at our phones and our social media.

After about ten minutes, I decided to go out back and step out for a smoke. I got up, grabbed a refill on my soda, and went out the back door where I could light up a cigarette and have some peace and quiet for five minutes alone. I stood there because there weren't any seats—no chairs or stools to relax on. I thought about Jen. I saw her grabbing her food in the kitchen window—her blond hair waving, pretty eyes looking over her plates and at her tickets—she was a dream. But I still wondered about Cecilia—this urge to call her would grow in the coming days. But right now, I needed to figure out how to get my dad's insurance so he could pay for his oxygen tank, medications, and the monthly visits to Dr. Ferguson's office. I was at a loss, but what could I do right at this moment? So, I threw my finished cigarette and walked back inside the Open House Bar and Grill without any solutions to my dad's problems or to my relenting issues. The burden was there—it would always be there.

6

Towards the end of the day, around three o'clock, I sat up front and waited for four to roll around. Jen came up to me. I was nervous.

"Hey," she said with a smile.

I said "Hey" back to her.

"I was just wondering if you wanted to go out some time again soon."

Was she asking me out?

"If not, it's cool, but I enjoyed the other night and— "

Terry walked up. "What are you guys talking about?" He was smirking.

"Nothing," I said. I turned to Jen. "Yes. I'd like that."

"Great!" She was happy. I was happy. She walked away and left me and Terry alone.

"What happened?" he asked me.

"I think she just asked me out for a second date."

"Oh, no shit? Terrific! I guess she had a good time on the first one then." He patted me on the back.

An hour later, we all clocked out for shift-change. I was ready to leave. *Shit.* I was ready over two hours ago. I got into my little car, lit up a smoke, and pulled away from the restaurant's parking lot. Again, I would go for my usual coffee before heading home.

7

On the way to the apartment from the coffee shop with the drink in my cup holder, I thought about what it would take to get my father back on insurance. I knew a little about all that, considering I had insurance for my medications and my own doctor. I wondered how much it would be to start a plan with my insurance for my father.

When I got home and settled in, I took out my phone and called my health insurance company. It rang a few times, then there was a prerecorded prompt. I dialed a few of the numbers, and it directed me to an operator.

"Hello. Thank you for calling Premier Health Insurance. How can I help you today?" the man on the other end of the line stated.

"Yes," I replied, "I'm looking to sign up my dad with you guys. I have Premier for myself, but I just wanted to see what it would take for him to get insurance through your company."

"Okay," the man said. "Great."

Eventually, I gave the representative all my dad's information— what I couldn't remember, I had to go to my dad's room and ask him for it—but after some time, the representative gave me the results. To start my dad today, at that moment, would be $475, and every month here after, would be $350. It might not seem much, but just myself supporting my father, it was a lot of money on top of all the other bills I already had to pay. I told the representative that I would think it over—because I didn't have the money right now—and I would call Premier Insurance back another time. I told the man to have a good day, and I hung up the line.

Shit.

I figured it was going to be a penny or two to get my dad insurance, but it was more expensive than I anticipated. I sat on my bed with phone in hand looking down. I was upset. I didn't want my father to be in pain.

After a moment, it came to me.

I could get a second job.

The days were long at the Open House restaurant, but I could do it if I really had to, which I did. I could work a second job for my dad's medical needs.

The rest of the night I spent on the internet looking at job boards for part-time work during the evenings. I would fall asleep again, fully clothed, phone on my chest.

6

Chapter 6

1

A couple of days after I started my search for a second job, I had an interview with a small "mom and pop" pizza restaurant. I worked my shift at the Open House, and then headed for the little pizza place down on Main Street. I pulled into the empty parking space in front of the building and peered out and up out of my front window. The sign up-top read "Mama Vici's Pizza & More". I got out of the car and looked at my reflection in the driver's side window. I fixed my hair a bit by running my hand through it and tucked in my shirt. I was still somewhat dirty from work. I didn't mind though. I wasn't too thrilled to be here anyhow.

Inside, I was greeted by a young and attractive Hispanic woman. She asked if I was dining in, and I told her I had an interview with the owner. She walked away and when she came back a small Mexican woman followed her. She looked worn—like the years had had their toll on her—but strong still.

"Samuel?" she asked with a smile, as she approached me.

I put out my hand to shake hers, said yes, and after a moment we sat down at a booth at the front of the restaurant. It smelt nice inside. It smelt of homemade pizzas, spaghetti sauce, and garlic bread sticks.

"We're looking for someone to help in the kitchen in the evenings," she said. "We need someone who knows their way around."

I stopped her there and replied, "I've been working in kitchens my whole life. I work at the Open House Bar and Grill, but I'm looking for extra work to make ends meet."

"Ah. Two jobs won't be too much on you?"

I could tell she was somewhat concerned. I needed the job. It *might* be too much, but I lied.

"I don't think so," I replied. "I can handle it."

She took a moment to think. My eyes wandered from the table to the pretty hostess that had greeted me earlier. I gazed at her body up and down while she faced away from us.

"When can you start?" the older woman asked.

2

I was lying on my bed later that evening. It was about 9 o'clock and Jen had text me. She wanted to set up another date. She was being persistent. I didn't know rather to like this or not, but I went with it. We talked about the movies, but I always fell asleep inside the theater watching them, and right now, there was really nothing playing that interested me. So, we settled on dinner and a walk.

I was very attracted to her, don't get me wrong, but I just couldn't get Cecilia out of my head. The vixen with the red hair and blond bangs had haunted me since the fender bender. I couldn't lose her out of my mind, even if I had wanted to.

I'm obsessed.

My phone buzzed again.

It was Jen again, and it read, *"How about tomorrow evening? Are you free then?"*

I laid my phone on my chest, closed my eyes, and my mind drifted to a place with Cecilia next to me at the coffee shop. In my head, she was standing next to me and laughing. Her smile was big, and I was blushing. We were talking over hot coffee. She told me about her past, I talked of the future, and we spoke of everything in between.

I must have fallen asleep because the following morning, I woke up with my phone by my side and I was on top of my blanket. I got out of bed and made my way to the kitchen to see if the coffee had been already made. If dad were awake, the coffee would be ready. If not, I'd have to stumble in there and brew it myself.

My father was awake. It was seven-thirty, and I made my way to grab a mug from the cabinet.

"Morning," he said, as I passed the couch.

"Hey," I replied. I was exhausted.

I grabbed a cup and poured the hot, black coffee into my mug, and after, took out the cream from the refrigerator to add to it. I realized it was a mug my mother used to drink out of when she was alive. It brought unwanted feelings back into my head—feelings off loss, hurt, and anger—I didn't know how to interpret them, so I put the mug back in the cabinet and grabbed another.

"Do you have to go to work this morning?" my dad yelled over the television, which played the news on the local station channel six.

"Yeah," I said. I had nothing but short answers right now as I was readying my cup.

"I needed to go to the grocery store," my father added. "I wanted to get a couple of things."

"I can take you after my shift."

"That'll be fine." He turned back to face the television and continued watching the news.

I dragged myself to the couch next to my dad. I sat and took out my phone. After a couple of sips, I unlocked the screen and opened the last message from Jen.

"*I guess you fell asleep. Alright. I hope we go out tomorrow. But anyway, I'll see you at work. Night.*"

I sat my phone on the coffee table.

"They say we're getting a new park in town," my dad said, pointing at the television. "Mayor's doing something finally."

I nodded and grinned. I was still very tired and wanted nothing more than to drink my coffee in peace and silence. My head was pounding and I'm sure my dad had been awake since five o'clock; he was an early riser. I kept sipping at my coffee for the next twenty minutes. I, too, looked at the flat screen and watched the segments covering our little town of Ingleside. The closest metro-city was

Corpus Christi, and it always had negative stories plastered throughout the morning show. It was depressing. City Officials *this*, CCPD *that*. I never really cared for it. I just wanted to wake up with my coffee in hand.

About nine, I got ready for work and headed out the door. Before I could get into my car, my phone rang.

"Hello?"

"Yes, hello, Samuel Williams?" the voice asked.

"Yes? Can I help you?"

"It's regarding the small wreck you had the other day with one 'Cecilia James'. It's her insurance company—we're waiting for your end to come through. We just wanted to reach out and make sure everything was okay and going smoothly."

Oh, shit …

I hopped into the Toyota. I should have taken care of this a while back.

"Yeah. I'm headed to work right now, but I'll call my insurance first thing on break. Okay?"

"Yes, Mr. Williams. Please do. Cecilia is trying to get her car into the auto shop and we're waiting for your side to go through."

Fuck.

"Alright," I replied, "I'll get on it this afternoon."

"Have a good day, Mr. Williams." They hung up.

I tossed my phone into the passenger seat and put the car in gear. I was off to work. I never did get rid of that headache.

3

I had told Mama Vici that I could start tonight, after my day shift with the Open House. Although I wasn't prepared to work all day until ten o'clock, I knew it was something I had to do for my dad. He needed health insurance, and his Social Security wasn't covering him anymore. It was up to me to pay the bills and keep us stable with the finances, and it was up to me to keep a roof over our heads, and it was up to me to keep us going. The burden of adulthood and self-maintenance was looming over me. I just wanted to throw every pan in the Open House against the wall and pull out my hair. It wasn't hard work. It might have been the responsibility. The feeling of dread maybe—like I might fail, and my dad might die because of me. It was daunting; it happened all the time for many and often covered on the morning news on channel six.

My day was going okay, but every time Jen's food was ready, and she would grab it from the window, I could feel her eyes on me. I wondered if she thought I had lost interest. It wasn't that—I was just growing ever so infatuated with the red-haired woman from the café. I felt like she was consuming me. I made up my mind during my shift to call her tonight when I got home.

I could say her insurance called me and I was just checking in. Yeah! That was a good opener. I could say something like, "Let's grab a coffee!" No, you fool. Stupid! She'll say no for sure to that line. Maybe tell her she's pretty?

A few hours had passed, and the lunch rush was over. I was sitting up front at our usual table with Greg and Terry when Jen came up to me.

"Hey, Sam. Um," she hesitated. I could tell my lack of engagement towards her lately was bothering her, "Did you still want to go out?"

I cleared my throat. "Oh, yeah. For sure," I replied. "I've got to work tonight though. I picked up a second job."

"Okay." She seemed annoyed but kept on. "Maybe after your shift tonight we could grab a drink? It doesn't have to be dinner," she said.

I thought it over for a second.

I would be tired. So tired.

But after a moment, I agreed to the drink tonight. She seemed happy now and excited. I guess I had taken away her worry. She hopped up and down after I said yes, then went back into the waitress station. I was reluctant though to go out. It would be a very long day. I know all I would want to do after Mama Vici's is to just go home.

Shit. Why did I say yes?

"Alright!" Terry said to me. "Got another date! Big man!"

I hated it when Terry butt-in like that. As much as I loved him, he got on my nerves too most of the time.

I sat and played around on my phone for another fifteen minutes then went out back to grab a smoke in solitude. I stood outside looking at the birds jump around and play with each other. I thought about how the rest of the day would go. I would leave here at four o'clock and I told the owner of Mama Vici's I would be in at five to start my shift there. I had been in restaurants all my life, but pizza would be a new venture for me. I had never made one. The fettuccine was no problem.   I could make pastas, but I would have to learn how to make the pizzas. I wasn't worried though. I was a quick learner and picked up fast. I was ready and I needed this for my dad. Without it, we couldn't afford what he needed to stay healthy and alive. I blinked and I was back smoking behind the restaurant. I took one last puff of the cigarette and flicked it away.

At four, I left and headed for Mama Vici's Pizza.

As I drove, I thought about how my life would play out now and what the future might hold for my dad and me. It was just the two of us for a long time—since mom had passed three years ago. I've got a brother, but that's another story.

What would happen to my father now?

I feared for the worst if I couldn't come up with the extra funds for his insurance. I thought about adding him to my insurance or signing him up with who I had for my medications.

Everything left my mind as I pulled into Mama Vici's. I parked and took off my seatbelt. I was forty-five minutes early. I sat there and peered out of the front windshield and looked inside the pizza restaurant. It wasn't busy right now. Two tables sat and ate their meals.

"Well," I said aloud, "Fuck it."

I got out of the car, jumped onto the sidewalk missing water sitting in the gutter of the curb, and made my way through the doors to the inside.

"Hey," the young Hispanic girl from before greeted me. "I don't think we met. I'm Nancy." She shook my hand. "Mrs. Garza is in the back if you want to head to the kitchen. I'll walk you."

"Sure," I replied. I followed behind her as she walked passed the tables and around the counter. We entered the kitchen.

The old woman from before smiled at me and held out her arms.

"Hola, Sam!" She hugged me. "Are you ready?"

I nodded.

"Apron?" she asked me.

I took the black apron from her grip and put it on.

"Now, you said you have never made pizza before?"

I guess it was *Mrs. Garza* and not *Mama Vici*.

She continued. "I will show you!"

4

After a few hours, and a couple pizzas later, I started to get the hang of everything. But it was time to grab a cigarette. So, I asked Nancy where I could go to step out for a smoke. She said there was a back door passed the dry storage and I could exit the building there. I would find a seat and table. Nancy told me Mrs. Garza smoked too, and that was the designated smoking area. I did as she told me. I was outside now and enjoying my first cigarette since being here.

My phone buzzed. I had a text alert. It was from Dad.

"Just checking on you, son. I thought you would be home by now."

I hadn't told him yet that I had picked up a second job.

I replied, *"I'll be home after a while. I've got a date tonight."*

Then, before I could put my phone back in my pocket, another message came through. It was from Jen.

"Hey. Let's meet at the Irish pub on Main. It's close by Mama's."

I wrote, *"Okay,"* then stuffed my phone back in my pocket.

I had a few more drags before my time ended outside.

5

It was the end of the night, Mama Vici's was closed, and I had just cleaned up the kitchen. I wrote my time down on a piece of paper and handed it to Nancy before I left the restaurant.

"See you tomorrow," she said.

I waved as I got into my car and headed for the Irish pub down the street. When I got there, I didn't see Jen outside.

I wrote to her. *"I'm outside in my car."* I waited for a reply.

A moment later, she got back to me with, *"I'll come out. Stay put!"*

I got out of my car and waited next to it. I saw her exit the bar.

46

She came to me.

"Hey!" she yelled, waving her arm.

I waved back. I said, "Hey," when she got in proximity. "Have you been waiting long?"

"No. About fifteen minutes, I guess."

"Okay."

I stood there and she looked up at me with a pretty smile. She was cute, but Cecilia was in my head—she was floating around inside there swimming and causing havoc. I spoke up and gestured to the door. "Should we go in?"

"Right," she let out. "Let's go!"

We walked side by side.

The music was loud. There was a time one could smoke in a bar—not anymore since the ordinance changed years ago. The bar smelt of perfume, hairspray, and whiskey. It wasn't my *scene*, but I did like the occasional beer. I didn't mind going out once in a blue moon. I was going to try to enjoy the night. But my mind was made up. Tomorrow, I would call Cecilia and try to make conversation some way or another.

We sat at a tall table on a couple of stools. A waitress approached.

"What can I get for you two?" she asked.

I looked at Jen and said, "Whatever you feel like."

"You're so nice." Jen smiled and ordered a house margarita on the rocks.

The waitress turned to me.

"I'll take a Bud please." I was simple. I didn't need much.

I had my arms crossed and I was leaning on the small round table. Jen had her blond hair up in a ponytail. Her neck looked pleasant and kissable. But no matter how much she appealed to me— the lingering thought of Cecilia still festered in my head.

I started to gaze around the room and my attention was not on Jen. I guess she could tell because after a moment she called out to me and woke me from my late-night trance.

"How was work?" she hollered above the music.

"What?" I asked her. It was difficult to hear in this place.

She repeated herself.

"Oh! It was fine," I replied.

The waitress brought our drinks, and said, "There you go, you two. If you all need anything else, don't hesitate to ask."

I really didn't want to be here. I wanted to smoke, and I was tired from the day. I wanted to go home and crawl into bed. But I continued the conversation anyway and amused Jen.

"How was your day?" I asked her, then took a drink of my beer. I leaned it back and took a big gulp. A small buzz wouldn't hurt. I needed something to kill the dry conversation. I hated small talk.

6

Two hours later, Jen and I were stumbling together out of the Irish pub on Main Street. We were laughing and holding each other close. I didn't know which foot was my right, and which was my left as I made my way to my car. Before I could get there, Jen stopped me and looked into my eyes. I looked down at her. She leaned into me and kissed me on the mouth. Although I didn't find her all that fascinating, I was lonely and returned the kiss.

"Come home with me," she said, then put her head on my chest squeezing me close to her body.

I looked around and even though I was hesitant, I held her just as close. In the moment, I agreed to follow her back to her place.

We got to an apartment complex on the other side of town. We parked and I followed her up to her apartment on the third story of the building. At the door, she was clumsy with her keys. We had a lot to drink at the bar. Finally, she opened the door, and we went inside. She began to kiss me on the lips. We moved across her living room floor together. I suppose we were making our way to the bedroom. She started to help me with my shirt. I unbuttoned her blouse. We entered the room. We parted. She started for her jeans. After a second, she was down to her underwear, and I was only in my pants and shoes. She grabbed me by the waist and pushed me to the bed. I lay there looking at her.

Jen reached behind her back and took off her bra. Her small breasts were round and pale. It had been some time since I had last seen a naked woman. I was aroused, but something was wrong. I still thought of Cecilia, the woman from the coffee shop, the woman who I had had a run-in with. Jen climbed on top of me. Her long blond hair cascaded down on my face like a waterfall of gold. My hands were on her thighs as she kissed me passionately. I felt her moist lips against mine. Her hot breath turned me on. It entered my mouth with each kiss. I could feel myself rubbing against Jen's panties. I wanted her, but, at the same time, I felt sick. It all felt wrong.

"I can't," I said, and pushed her away.

She got off of me and was on the bed on her knees now.

"What's wrong?" Jen asked me.

"Nothing," I replied. "Too much beer, I guess."

She looked so disappointed. I had hurt her.

I didn't have much to say, and so I picked up my shirt from off the floor and put it on. At her doorway, I looked back at her before leaving the room. She looked sad and confused. She wanted to cry. I could tell. I turned and left. I didn't have anything to say but goodbye.

7

Chapter 7

1

The next day as I was clocking in for my shift at the Open House restaurant, I decided to call Cecilia that evening when I got home. I would be free. Mrs. Garza didn't need me that night at Mama Vici's pizza restaurant. I decided I would call her up, maybe start with the whole *insurance* thing, then ease my way into her heart with more flatteries and compliments perhaps. I could tell her how beautiful I think she is. I could tell her she has a pretty smile. Then, she would probably tell me to pay up. I really couldn't afford to fix her bumper out of pocket. I hoped my insurance would cover the damage. I got a drink then walked to the kitchen to get my day started.

I sat my drink down on the stainless-steel table, said good morning to Greg and Terry, and made my way to the walk-in cooler. I looked around for things I needed to prep today. There was rice that was made the night before that needed to be portioned, of course we needed hamburger patties, and calamari could be portioned too. I walked out and back to the kitchen.

Terry stopped me, and he asked, "How did last night go with Jen?"

"Don't ask," I replied.

"That bad. Huh? It's okay. You can't win them all. But it really seemed like you two would hit it off. Sorry, man."

And that was just it. We did "hit it off". But deep down, I didn't want her, I wasn't really interested in pursuing anything with the young waitress, Jen. I had other plans in my head. Cecilia had captured me, and I had grown infatuated. I wanted to know her and see what she was about. I wasn't good at juggling women, and so I made up my mind to leave Jen alone ... only if she would leave me alone.

2

Thirty minutes later, on the line, the rush was beginning—the sizzle of the fryers as I dropped waffle fries into them, the steam coming off the grill as Greg dropped hamburger patties onto it ... the kitchen was alive. Tickets started to come in. The printer screaming, "Pluck these tickets!" The energy was high. As each order rolled in, Greg would pull the carbon paper ticket, keep his white copy, and hand me the yellow copy with the exact same order on it. Waffle fries, curly fries, tater tots ... I would put everything in the baskets as it came in. One basket of a side would be ready, and I would dump it into the silver bowl until I was ready to plate it with Greg's burger or chicken wings. I would hand these plates off to Terry, who was the expo. His job was to finish the plates off with a side of ranch, or, if it were a hamburger, he would add lettuce, tomatoes, or pickles and onions. The overhead vents would inhale all the smoke and steam coming off Greg's grill and breathe life as we hurried to get everything out in a timely manner—this went on for two and a half hours until about one thirty in the afternoon.

Finally, it was over.

Greg scraped off the grill as I threw the cold remaining fries into the trash.

"Sam," he said.

"Yeah?"

"I'm moving."

"What do you mean?" I asked, puzzled.

"I already told the boss. I'm moving up to Odessa with the

family and I won't be working here any longer."

I was saddened. I worked with Greg the last two years. Up until now, he had been a good mentor to me and a great coworker. I was blindsided by this news. He hadn't mentioned it prior to this.

"The boss wants you to run the kitchen for the lunch shifts," he said to me. He stopped scraping the grill and turned to me. "I know you can do it. You have watched me do everything. You can do it."

I stopped what I was doing and set the stainless-steel bowl down. "I guess, if you say so, man," I replied.

Greg started to scrape the grill again. He said, "I put in my two weeks yesterday. So. There. Now you know."

I was disappointed he wouldn't be with us anymore. But I understood.

3

When I got home later that afternoon, I walked inside and greeted my dad. He was sitting on the couch as usual watching the early five o'clock news. He muttered at each story and sipped on his sweet tea.

"How was work?" he asked me, as I made my way into the kitchen to grab a glass of water.

I hollered from a distance over the television, "It was fine!"

"Good, son," he replied. He was a man of little words, but when he did say something, they were profound.

"I'm going to my room."

I cracked the window inside my room and lit a cigarette. I usually stepped out onto the patio area, but I was tired today and wanted to lay down. I kicked off my shoes and put up my feet. I laid there and looked up at the ceiling, and then my eyes switched over to the table beside my bed. Cecilia's number still lay on top of it. It was crinkled, but the name and number legible still after a few days.

I should try. I should try calling her.

I fished out my cell from my left front pocket and grabbed the piece of paper with her number on it. I dialed in the number, but I hesitated to press the "Call" button.

What if I creep her out? Maybe start off with the insurance claim?

I hadn't even talked to my insurance company yet.

Maybe tell her you saw her the other day? No, you idiot, that is creepy!

I put the phone with the screen closed on my bedside table and laid there still staring upwards. I picked it up, then put it back down. This went on for the next half hour. Finally, I gathered the courage to press the little green button in the shape of a phone and managed to get the phone ringing. I waited.

Ring, ring …ring, ring … ring, ring.

She picked up the line and said, "Hello?"

Fear stricken, I hung up. I had pressed the "End Call" button so fast that I hadn't given her a chance to follow up with her greeting.

Such a wimp!

I put the phone down back onto the little table that stood beside me. It started to ring.

Shit, shit, shit!

I looked at the screen and it was Cecilia calling back.

What the hell do I do?! Answer, you fool!

I grabbed the phone and answered the call.

"Hello?"

"Hello. I had a missed call from this number," she stated.

Her voice was recognizable and pretty—it was heavy, but quaint and gentle, feminine, whilst being somewhat deep also.

"Yeah, hi … it's … it's Sam," I managed to get out, "From the other day—the guy that wrecked into you." I waited a moment for some kind of recognition. A response. But all was silent. "Do you remember me?" I asked her.

"Yes, of course," she said, at last, "I remember."

I was thrilled.

But then she said, "I have a huge dent in my bumper because of you."

Shit. That's not good.

But, of course, it *was* my fault, after all.

"Were you able to get your insurance situated?" she asked.

Why did I call this woman?

"I … I … Uh … Haven't yet, no. I wanted to talk it over with you first." I was lying. "I wanted to get your opinion on a few things." I was pulling it out my ass.

"Okay?"

I could tell she was growing annoyed that I had not come to a solution for her busted up bumper. She didn't answer or return the call to talk about going out. She wanted results, she wanted me to fix it, she wanted a new fucking bumper!

"Maybe we should meet?" I blurted out.

What the fuck was that?

"Because …" I added, "It might be easier to take care of all of this face to face, in person. You know?"

"True," she said. "I can meet tomorrow."

"How about Friday instead?" I replied. I was working at the Open House and Mama Vici's tomorrow. I wouldn't have time, even in between shifts. "I can't tomorrow."

"Yes. Friday is good."

I could have fallen deep in love with her just over these past few minutes. Her voice alone captured me.

You are one love-sick puppy. Better stop drooling. Wipe your chin, Sam!

"At the coffee shop?" I continued. "And I promise I won't bump into you this time."

She chuckled.

Look at that! I got a laugh. Good one, buddy!

"Yes. Friday at the coffee shop is fine. I've got to go now. But I'll see you then," she said.

I said bye and hung up the phone. I was smitten. I couldn't wait for the next day to pass. I had a date with Cecilia.

Yeah, but it's to talk about insurance and shit. But you never know. There could be a slight chance I might sweep her off her feet and we would ride away in her SUV with the dented bumper. It could happen!

I placed my phone down, put my hands under my head, and looked up at the ceiling again.

I hoped it would go well.

4

I must have fallen asleep.

I woke up the next morning fully clothed—socks, jeans, and shirt on from the day before.

What time is it?

I picked up my phone. It read "seven-thirty". Besides that, I had a text from Jen and my boss, Emilio.

Emilio came from money and owned a string of restaurants throughout Ingleside and the surrounding towns. He was young, good-looking, and had—what seemed—the perfect life. I had to admit when I first started, I was a little jealous. But as time went on, I came to respect him. He was a good boss and ran a tight ship. I could respect that. But, man, what a life he had! If only I could live a day in those shoes.

I opened Jen's text first.

"Hey, Sam. I hope we're okay. You seem distant since the night we almost slept together. I'm sorry if I scared you off. I didn't mean to. I hope we can at least be friends and stay civil coworkers. I don't want it to be weird between us at work. Shoot me a message, or I'll see you tomorrow. I work lunch. Bye!"

Then, I opened Emilio's text.

"Sam, can you come in early? I need to discuss something with you. Be in at eight o'clock."

"Shit!" I yelped. I had thirty minutes to get down to the Open House. I wondered if this was about Greg. I had gotten a raise about six months ago. There's no way he wanted to raise my pay. Or did he? An official title would be cool. I wasn't looking to be in charge, but I would step up to the plate if he needed me to. In a frantic whirlwind, I put on my shoes, shoved my smokes in my pocket and took up my keys. I was out the door in a minute flat. I hauled ass in my little Toyota coupe down Main Street and hit the highway. After ten minutes of dodging cars and zooming from lane to lane, I got to the Open House just in time. Emilio's truck was parked in the lot. I jumped out as quickly as I could and hurried for the front door.

I got inside and could see his office door was open. I kept a cool, calm, and collected attitude as I headed his way. I knocked on the wall.

"Hey. You wanted to see me, Emilio?"

"Yes, yes. Come in!" he replied, waving his hand inward.

There was only his desk chair inside. No seat for me. So, I stood.

"Sam," he said, starting off strong with a professional voice, "You've been a big help here and an asset to the growth of this restaurant. I respect that and I'm grateful."

Okay, okay. Get on with it.

"I want you to take over Greg's shifts," he said, "And I'm going to bump up your pay for taking on that responsibility."

I smiled, and said, "Yes, sir."

"I feel like you can handle it. You up for it?" He smiled too.

"Yes," I replied. "I can handle it. No problem."

"Great! That's all, Sam." He was finished.

I said thank you and left his office. I went to grab a quick smoke. I was thrilled and excited and more motivated than before. I was ready to take this next step. I was overwhelmed with pride and feelings of glee. I had reached a point I had been longing for. This was a new chapter, and I felt great about it. I felt like I could take on the world. I finished my smoke quickly because Emilio was still there and I didn't like to smoke when he was present in the building. I clocked in for my lunch shift. I was floating the whole rest of the morning and into the afternoon.

5

After lunch, about an hour before I was able to leave, Jen walked up to me.

"Hey," she said, with a sad look in her eyes. "I sent you a text last night. You never replied."

I knew she was disappointed.

"I saw this morning. I fell asleep early last night," I replied. "I'm sorry. But I agree. We should stay friends. And for what it's worth you didn't scare me off. I'm just not ready." It was partly true. My last relationship didn't go so well. I was with a woman nine years older than me who only wanted to be loved by anyone I came to think after we broke up, and I couldn't reciprocate that feeling. It ended after a year. It ended six months ago, in fact. I wasn't ready to pursue anyone—except for Cecilia that is. Jen nodded her blond head then went about her duties. I felt miserable. But what could I do? I had learned over time that counterfeit feelings led me nowhere except for pain. I didn't want to do that to myself again.

Terry walked up and sat down next to me. He folded his arms on top of the table and laid his head in them. He dozed off after a few minutes. I looked up at the big screen television and watched a rerun of the Astros baseball game. Before I knew it, I was out of there and at Mama Vici's.

The little pizza restaurant was easier, and I often worked alone, which I didn't mind. It was, for the most part, pasta and large pizzas with miscellaneous toppings. On the occasion, I would get a standard pepperoni pizza, but the adults seemed to like "Supreme" most of the time. I enjoyed making them. It was easy work. And I still had to figure out what I was going to do for my father and his dilemma.

After Mama Vicia's closed, I drove away in my Toyota and made my way home.

I would meet Cecilia and get to talk to her tomorrw. I was excited. Besides my father's situation, things were looking up. Maybe it would all work out, as my father would often tell me if I was ever stressed or in trouble.

I got into the apartment, and again, my dad was past out in front of the television. The shows from the '60s era were on. Reruns for older people—seniors—that enjoyed watching television from their youth. *The days had gone by way too fast.*

I grabbed the remote and turned it off. I put a blanket on my dad and nestled one of the pillows on the couch under his head.

"Love you, dad," I whispered, then went to my room for the night.

As I went to bed and started to slip away, I thought of Cecilia's voice, her face, the possibilities of my new responsibilities at the restaurant, and a faraway land where, in time, dreams do come true.

8

Chapter 8

1

It was Friday, and I was ready to meet with Cecilia that afternoon.

I was off work and had a few errands to run before, however. I needed to get groceries. That was the important one—the main task of the day. I decided to go early. So, about eight in the morning, I headed for the store to pick up what we needed for over the weekend. My dad loved to make himself a couple of chili dogs while I was at work. I needed to get him more buns and chili. It was inexpensive and easy for him to heat up without me there at the apartment. I pushed the cart around the little grocery store and added slowly as I went down each aisle. I had about a hundred bucks to spend. So, I didn't get too many items. I didn't want to get anything useless or that might spoil quickly.

After I was done at the store, I went to the post office and dropped off some mail. I had to get stamps. I didn't mind. It was cheap. I sent off two pieces of mail and left. Now, I headed for an outlet store. I needed new non-slip shoes for work. Mine had been worn. They were over a year old and tearing at the sole.

I was sitting on a bench in the shoe section of the store and looking at a pair of black non-slips. An associate of the store walked by me, and I quickly grabbed their attention.

"Excuse me!" I waved at them. "Do you have this in a size fifteen?" I asked. I had always had big feet. My shoe size blew up when I hit puberty as a young man.

"I'm not sure," they said. "I'll go check the back."

A few minutes later, the twenty-something-year old man came back with a box in his hands. "Try these," he said.

I opened the box, and the shoes were blue and red. A little *loud* for my taste, but after trying them on, and feeling how comfortable they were, I bought them.

"Thank you," I said to him as I took up the box and headed for the exit.

I still had hours before the meeting with Cecilia. So, to kill some time, I ordered take-out breakfast for dad and myself. I picked it up from a small diner on the edge of town. It was about fifteen minutes away from the apartment. They had good eggs.

I returned home, at last, with a bag in hand, which had breakfast.

"Dad, come and eat!" I hollered. I guessed he had made his way to his room in the middle of the night and now lay in bed. I hoped he wasn't asleep. I didn't want his fifteen-dollar plate to get cold and eventually thrown away. "Dad!" I yelled once again. I sat the bag down on the kitchen counter and headed for his bedroom. "Dad?"

My dad turned over. He was on his side. He lifted his head and looked at me. "Son, it's early," he muttered.

"I bought breakfast. Come and get it while I bring in the groceries."

"Oh, you went to the store?"

"Yes. Now, come on before it gets cold."

My dad lifted himself up and out of bed. He was wearing his pajama bottoms and a plain white tee. His hair disheveled and stuck outward in different directions. He rubbed his eyes as he came out of his room.

"It's on the counter," I told him. "You've got the bacon. I believe yours is the top box."

"Yeah, yeah, yeah …" he muttered some more, as he untied the plastic bag.

I headed back to the car to get the groceries. It took about four trips to get everything inside. The stairs were killer by the third round. After my last trip, I sat the bags on the dining table. Dad was already digging into his breakfast from the little diner that sat on the edge of town.

"Is this Sarah's?" he asked.

"Yes, dad. Sarah's Diner."

Sarah was a middle-aged woman who, after her husband passed and collected life insurance, decided to open her own restaurant. It prospered after a slow start. She did well for herself.

"Good, good," he replied, whilst chewing on a slice of crisp bacon.

I told my dad as I put away the groceries, "I've got a meeting today. Are you going to be alright without me for a few hours this afternoon?"

He looked over his shoulder at me. "I usually am while you're at work, aren't I?"

"Good point," I replied.

After I finished putting the groceries away, I got my breakfast plate and sat next to my dad on the couch. My eggs were cold, sausage patty over cooked … it wasn't so great by the time I got to start on it.

"Can you believe they got Mitchell to resign his mayor position?" Dad shook his head. "What a schmuck!"

He enjoyed "News at Noon"—one of my father's pass-times. I, on the other hand, enjoyed a simple cigarette on the patio of the apartment, and listened to the sounds of the street and outside. There were two trees by the balcony where birds would sit and chirp. It was peaceful. I enjoyed sitting outside. Maybe why I continued to smoke regularly. Because I liked to be out and needed an excuse to be there for five minutes at a time. It might look strange if I just sat there and did nothing. I would look like a nut!

2

After breakfast, I took a short nap. It lasted about an hour and a half. I sat up on my bed and opened my phone. No texts and no missed calls while I slept.

The time read two o'clock. I was to meet Cecilia at three. I had an hour, and so I grabbed some fresh clothes and took a shower. One thing about working in restaurants was that you would always sweat during your shift. It was guaranteed. I dressed myself after and put on my shoes. I took up my phone, keys, and smokes and headed out the door. But before I did, my dad said, "I love you," and I patted him on the shoulder.

"I'll be back soon," I told him, and left.

I got to the coffee shop about fifteen minutes before three. I didn't see her SUV. So, I sat in my car and waited a moment.

What was I going to say to her?

I would fall short. I was supposed to report good news, not bad. I hadn't called my insurance company and filed a claim. I was slacking. I sat there gripping the wheel. Sweaty palms and a wet forehead, I grew worried and anxious.

I should have taken an anxiety pill. It would have helped, Sammy boy!

I decided to get out and go inside. I ordered my usual almond milk and light cream. I found a table and took a seat. Hands drenched, they held onto the large, insulated coffee cup with a cardboard sleeve. I looked out the window and waited for Cecilia to show. After some time had gone by, and she never showed up, I got up and went outside for a smoke. I stood there, coffee in one hand and cigarette in the other. My phone buzzed in my pocket.

"Hey. It's Cecilia. Not going to make it," she wrote. "I'm sorry. We'll have to get together another time. Or you can call me later. Let me know what you find out. Thanks."

In an odd way, I was relieved. She couldn't get here today. It was good because I had nothing to offer and no solutions to her dented bumper. I had escaped an awkward conversation. I didn't know what I would say. I sighed and put my phone back in my front pocket.

I threw the cigarette down and snuffed it out with my new shoe.

Way to go, Sam.

I got in my car and left.

3

Maybe I should call my insurance.

I was driving back to the apartment.

I was off from both jobs today and had plenty of time to call and settle with the insurance company. I needed to get it resolved in a timely manner before Cecilia found out and had a fit. I didn't want that. I wanted her to like me.

I got to my apartment and parked.

I sat there in the car for a moment and thought that maybe it was for the best that we hadn't met today. I had nothing to offer her. She wouldn't be interested in me.

Don't be so hard on yourself.

I got out of my Toyota and made my way upstairs to the second floor. I entered the apartment and dad was sitting on the couch still.

"Hey! You're back!" he yelled loudly. His words muffled through his oxygen mask.

"Hey, Dad," I said back.

I sat down next to him defeated.

"What's wrong, Son?" he asked me.

"Dad, how do you know if a woman likes you?" I asked him.

He laughed a bit. His oxygen mask fogged from his breath. "Son," he began, "Don't you think you're a little *old* to ask me something like that?"

I shook my head. "It's silly," I said. "Sorry." I tried to get up, but my dad grabbed my shoulder and sat me back down.

"Son, when I met your mother, I was very nervous. It took time to work up the courage to ask her out. I was scared. I'll admit that. But the day she said yes was the best day of my life. She agreed to go out with me one Saturday, and we never looked back after that."

"Right," I said.

"Doesn't exactly answer your' question, but if you like a woman and feel yourself drawn to her, then you should at least try to see if she likes you too. If you never know, you never will know."

Smart man.

I nodded then got up. I was going to go to my room and text Cecilia back. I'm sure I could pull something out of my ass to get the conversation going.

I sat on the edge of my bed holding my phone for a moment.

I opened my phone and brought up her text. I wrote in the text box, *"Hey,"* then sent it to the cosmos hoping it would reach her. I hoped she would get back to me quickly.

I realized then that I knew nothing about her: I didn't know what she did for work, who her friends were, what she was interested in—I just knew she enjoyed writing in journals at coffee shops and hated fender benders with strangers. I could understand that.

My phone buzzed in my hand.

I looked down and it was a reply from her. It read, *"Hey."*

Before I could think and scare myself into not replying, I wrote, *"It's Sam. It's okay that you couldn't meet today. I understand. Rain check?"*

After another few moments, she returned the message, and said, *"Yes! Next week?"*

"How about over a drink?" I wrote.

This time, it took a few minutes to get a response. But finally, I received, *"Are you asking me out?"*

I hesitated, and then wrote, *"Maybe?"*

"Lol. Yes, a drink is fine. But don't read too much into it. You did crash into me. Remember?"

I stood up quick like a bolt of lightning striking from the heavens.

"Yes!" I said aloud.

"Text me later to arrange it," she added. *"I'm at work right now."*

I fumbled my phone. After gathering myself and regaining control, I finished with, *"Yes. I'll text you later this evening. Have a good day, Cecilia."* I almost added a smiling emoji, but I stopped myself and simply sent what I had written. I sat back down.

Atta boy, Sammy!

4

I guess I had fallen asleep. I woke up and it was six o'clock. I rubbed my eyes and made my way out of my room.

"Dad?" I managed to say, still tired and exhausted.

"Sam, Sam … did you know we're getting a new skatepark for the rollerbladers and skateboarders next year?"

He was watching the evening news. He enjoyed staying up to date.

"Are you hungry?" I asked him. "I can go get us something to eat."

"And not only that ..." he continued, "But that stupid idiot Sheriff resigned after they found him sleeping with another officer. I guess he had to for appearances sake. Not exactly like they could *fire* him."

"Right," I said. "Burgers it is."

I went to my room, put on my shoes, and grabbed my keys. A moment later, I was out the door and headed to the nearest fast-food joint to grab us dinner.

On my drive there, I smoked a cigarette and thought how lucky I was that Cecilia had agreed to go have a drink with me. I was just a casual guy and didn't have much to offer. I still wasn't sure if Cecilia agreed to go out because she was interested in me or because she wanted her bumper fixed. No matter what the case, I was excited to meet with her. Whether over drinks, dinner, or even mini-golf, I was thrilled.

5

Later that evening after dinner, I was sitting on my bed. I was ready to text Cecilia and arrange the date. I saw it going well: meet up at a bar, go inside, get some drinks after finding a table, some laughing, some flirting, then after a few hours exit the bar, and finally a kiss goodnight before getting into our cars. Now, that was the ideal situation. If it would go like that, I didn't know. But one could only hope.

"*Hey,*" I wrote.

I stared at the screen for a moment. No reply. So, I sat the phone down on my bedside table. I looked around, sighed, then laid down. I had my arms crossed and feet up. I waited.

Maybe she was tired from work? She did say she had work today. I'm sure she'll get back to me in a bit.

My phone went off.

Yes! I was excited once again.

I opened my phone. It was Terry from work.

Shit!

"*Where did you put the left-over chicken?*"

Really, Terry?

The world depended on a text back from Cecilia, and I got a text from Terry instead. I was annoyed. I wrote back to him and told him where to find the chicken, which was cut up and stored in a container properly labeled and in plain-sight, I'm sure.

Terry, go away!

"*Thanks!*" he replied.

Piss off!

I lay in bed for an hour before I heard back from Cecilia. She finally wrote to me after waiting and feeling like the time had dragged.

"*Woo, what a day,*" she had written.

"*Long day at work?*"

"*Oh, yes.*"

I could feel myself smiling. I wanted to get down to business. So, I wrote, "*How about tomorrow night? We can meet up.*"

Another moment went by waiting.

Then, she wrote, "*I can do that. Time?*"

Yes!

I made a fist with my hand and shook it in the air.

On a roll, Sammy boy!

"*Nine sound good to you?*" I typed, then sent it into the nether that was the space that held so many texts like mine. Just into the air, I supposed messages went, but somehow got to their destinations. Obviously created by men much smarter than I.

"*Nine is great.*"

I was smitten. I hoped to win her over and woo her heart. She was more than I could have ever asked for. She was smart and pretty. I liked that.

"*Okay. I'll talk to you tomorrow then.*"

I sat my phone on my chest and buried my head in my pillow. The second pillow on my bed, I wrapped my arm around and pretended it was Cecilia.

9

Chapter 9

1

It was the next day, and I found myself in a good mood when waking up. I had work at the Open House Bar and Grill today, but I was off from Mama Vici's tonight. I scooted off the bed and put my feet on the ground. The carpet was in my toes and tickled a bit. I pushed my hands through my hair and wiped my eyes. I was tired, but pleasant.

The time read seven-thirty when I looked at my phone's screen. I had to be up at the restaurant at nine. I had a little time. So, I decided to go and make a pot of coffee.

Dad was awake and watching the news again.

"Sam, they've got a 'Wings Deluxe' coming to town next year," he said, as I strolled past the living room and into the kitchen.

I replied, "Great," then headed for the coffee maker.

Dad placed his oxygen mask on his face and went about his business watching the morning news that ran twice. He enjoyed staying up to date on Ingleside's upcoming events, opening and failing businesses, and a who's-who list of stories. He liked the small things in life in his older years and that made me feel good.

"Do you want some coffee, Dad?" I asked from the kitchen.

"I suppose I'll take a cup," he replied. "I had a pot earlier. But I'm ready for more."

I filled up the coffee pot with cool water and poured it into the back after filling the maker with coffee grounds. I pressed the *on* button and walked away to have a seat next to Dad while I waited for the coffee to ready.

"Not only are we getting a 'Wing Deluxe', but a new 'general store' as well!" My dad was thrilled at the new developments coming to our little town—the news covered the major city for the most part.

I could hear the coffee nearing its finish—gurgling and breathing. The apartment was filled with the aroma of fresh brewed coffee.

"Do you want me to get your cup, Dad?"

"Sure," he replied, not taking his sights off the television screen.

I got up and made my way into the kitchen. I dug out two mugs from the cupboard and a spoon from the drawer. I used liquid creamer, but Dad preferred the powder, which I kept up top next to the mugs. A little sugar for Dad, with creamer, and a bit of mine for my cup. I poured the coffee slowly into each mug. After, I walked them over to the coffee table in the living room area.

"Thanks, Sam," Dad said, with a smile beneath his mask. He lowered it. It hung around his neck. He picked up his mug and took a long, slow sip. "That's good, Son."

I followed suit and sipped at my cup.

We sat for half an hour and watched the news until it finished. After, the station played morning game-shows where contestants competed for cash prizes and money.

I got up and headed to my room. I grabbed my clothes and headed for the bathroom to shower. Working at a restaurant, a daily shower was necessary—even twice a day—to eliminate the odor of cooked food and the lingering scent of cooking grease on one's skin.

I got out and dressed. I got my keys and smokes. My phone had no messages and no missed calls. I had hoped Cecilia might text me this morning. I hoped we would still go out tonight together. I reassured myself that we were, but she could cancel like she did the last time; it wasn't improbable. I headed for the door.

"See ya, Dad!" I hollered as I left.

I heard a muffled reply, but I didn't know what he said. I

guessed he had said *goodbye* also, but I wasn't sure. Down the stairs and to my coupe. I got in and started the engine. Before I put the car in reverse, my phone went off with a notification. I pulled it out.

It read, *"Good morning! See you tonight!"* It was from Cecilia.

Yes!

I hit my clenched fist on the steering wheel. She had been thinking of me.

I replied, *"Good morning. I'm excited for tonight."*

I backed the car from my usual spot and headed to work.

2

I walked into the Open House Bar and Grill and clocked into the computer. I poured myself a tall cup of water and placed a lid on top of the cup. But before I could go back into the kitchen, Jen approached me.

"Hey, Sam," she said. "I was thinking we might try again and go out soon?"

I was blindsided and hesitated to answer her. I wasn't at all interested in the short, blond waitress anymore; I wasn't even sure if I wanted to be *just friends.*

I gathered my thoughts, and replied, "I don't think that's a good idea, Jen. I'm not really looking to date right now."

"But we went out," she said.

"I know, but that was an exception. I do find you attractive, but I'm just not ready, I think." I was pulling whatever I could out of my ass. "You're very sweet. But I just can't right now."

She lowered her head.

Was she crying?

"I'm sorry," I said, and placed my hand on her shoulder.

"Why does this always happen to me?" she said, with tears strolling down her soft, round cheeks. "I'm never good enough. I'm always the second choice—second best. I can't ever please *anyone!*"

I didn't know what else to tell her. So, I left her there alone. I walked to the back and into the kitchen area. Terry greeted me. I guess he caught some of what happened.

"What did you do?" he laughed. "You broke the poor girl's

heart."

"I know, I know," I replied, "I'm sure she'll get over me—over it. I'm nobody. She can do better."

"Don't sell yourself short," Greg interjected. "Even though I'm a big guy," he said, "I've gotten plenty of love from the opposite sex, if you know what I mean."

A little disturbed, I replied, "Thanks for that image, Greg. I'll go vomit now."

He laughed and walked away to the walk-in cooler.

"Sam," Terry continued, "Jen was hot. You're an ass and very stupid for letting that one go."

"You might be right," I said, "But I've got to do what feels right. And after my last girlfriend, Jen didn't feel right. I can tell now."

Terry was a couple years older than me, and I guess in his mind, that made his experiences more profound and credible, like he had all the advice in the world to share with me. He treated me more like his younger brother than a friend or coworker. He was always looking out for me. But sometimes his advice steered me wrong, and it was annoying to think he had anything substantial to add to my life. My troubles were mine, and mine alone, and no one could fix them for me. I had to go with the flow and ride the surf out myself. I couldn't rely on anyone. Not even my own father. I took care of *Dad*. There was a time when I was young and he watched over me, but now I was the caretaker and covered all the bills, cleaned the house, and looked after my father. I was in charge.

3

It was a few minutes away from the restaurant opening. I had just finished the hamburger patties—weighing them out and then shaping them into circles. I placed them all into a pan and put them away into the walk-in cooler after dating them.

When I walked back into the kitchen, Jen was standing there waiting for me.

"Hey," she said, "I know you don't want to go out, but I really think you should reconsider."

Terry was looking at me over her shoulder. His eyes were wide.

I knew he wanted to instigate the matter, but I hoped he wouldn't. This is exactly why I had avoided dating anyone from work for the past ten years—it always led to trouble.

"I'm a catch," she continued. "I'm attractive and smart. I don't see why you won't see me. You know you like me."

I did nothing but stand there surprised. I didn't have time for this. All the refinery workers would pour into the restaurant soon and place their orders. She should be up front getting ready herself. But she was here, with us, and causing trouble. She was frantic.

"I—I think you should give me another chance," Jen said. "At least a drink. Please?"

"Jen," I said, "I already told you earlier …"

"Yeah, but …"

"I just can't," I replied. I was feeling frustrated. "I shouldn't."

"You didn't even see if you really liked me or not. I know you have feelings for me, Sam."

She was unrelenting and pushy at this point.

I walked past her and to my station.

Greg was at the grill. He put down the spatula and looked at her. "Jen," he said, "You're going to have to leave the kitchen now. I'm sorry, but the restaurant is open, and I can't have you in the kitchen distracting my workers."

She stomped a foot and then left. I suppose she was more frustrated than I was. I looked at Greg and said, "Thanks."

He replied, "You owe me one."

I smiled.

"You've done it again, Sammy," Terry said, and then snickered.

4

The rush today was hectic. Greg was sending out burger after burger. I was hurrying to keep up and fix the plates with French fries, or tots, or sweet fries. I would ready the plate then pass it to Terry. He would then finish off the burgers with lettuce, tomato, pickles, and onions. If it was a chicken fried steak, I would batter it and then place it into the fryer in the vacant spot. If it was a chicken sandwich, it was like making the burgers. For chicken wings, Greg would put them in the basket and fry them, then it was up to me to put the flavored sauce on them and hand the plate over to Terry. Each plate of chicken wings came with a side of ranch dressing to dip the wings. The lunch rush was crazy today. But after two hours, it began to slow down.

We all started to clean up and wipe down the counters. The sauce bowls for the wings went to the dish-pit and any dirty plates would go into the sink as well. I threw out my trash and when I came back in, the manager, Vanessa, was waiting for me in the kitchen.

"Sam," she said, "Can I have a moment with you?"

I followed her to the office.

She sat down behind the sturdy desk. She looked up at me and said, "It's come to my attention that you and Jen have been seeing each other."

I replied, "Not exactly."

"What do you mean? She claims you two have been going out."

"Once," I retorted.

"Well," she continued, "She's very upset because, I guess, it didn't go well. She wants to be transferred to night shifts only. She doesn't want to work with you. She says she *can't.*"

This Jen bitch is crazy.

"I see," I said.

"You can't date the staff, Sam. It leads to this kind of stuff, and it makes it hard on me to schedule the girls. She was supposed to be a day-time server. Now, I've got to sort this whole mess out. See what happens?"

I didn't know what to say. So, I just nodded.

"You can leave now, Sam," Vanessa said, leaving it at that.

I left the office and headed back to my station to clean. I was confused. Jen is the crazy one, yet I got in trouble.

Bullshit.

"What happened?" Terry asked as soon as he saw me.

"Apparently, I'm a bad date," I replied.

I grabbed a wet towel and began wiping the steel table down that was stained with flour and Buffalo sauce.

"Jen made a complaint against me," I said. "The bitch is crazy and full of it. We went on *one* date and now she wants to be put on nights."

"No shit?"

"Yeah. She's psycho."

Terry picked up a towel also and started to wipe the opposite end of the table.

"Sounds psycho," he said, in disbelief.

10

Chapter 10

1

I was getting ready for my date with Cecilia later that evening. I was looking in the mirror making sure my shirt wasn't wrinkled and my hair looked all right. I was self-conscious and wanted to impress her.

Although she wanted to talk about insurance and how I could fix her bumper, I wanted to get to know Cecilia and make her laugh. I wanted her to like me. I wanted her to fall in love with me and maybe become obsessed. I just wanted a chance and it had been a very long time since I had a girlfriend. It would be nice to share moments and laughs with someone again. I was looking forward to tonight and I didn't want to mess anything up. It had to be perfect.

I wrote a text to her.

"Meet me at Hannah's Inn at nine. The lounge part on the side of the building. We can get a drink there."

Cecilia didn't respond right away, and that was okay. I fixed my hair, brushed my teeth, and put on deodorant and some cologne to smell good for her. I was groomed and ready to meet. But Cecilia hadn't replied yet. So, I sat on the edge of my bed and played on the phone until she confirmed our meeting place.

Finally, my phone went off and I looked down at it.

"Okay. I'll be there."

I jumped up and was thrilled.

Hell yeah, Sammy boy!

By now, it was almost eight o'clock, and Dad was sure to be hungry. So, I went out into the living room and asked him what he wanted for dinner.

"What do you feel like, Sam?" he replied.

"I'm actually going out tonight, Dad," I told him.

"Oh?"

"I've got somewhat of a date." I was awkward and avoided eye contact with him.

"Terrific," he said. "I guess I could just get a burger, Son. Nothing special. With mayo, please."

"Got it," I replied, then headed out the door with my smokes and keys in hand.

I went down to a burger place and got Dad his usual single patty with all the vegetables and mayo, no mustard. As I waited in the drive-thru line, my phone went off in my pocket.

I looked at the message. It was from Cecilia.

"Can we move it up to eight thirty? I'm ready now."

I would have to hurry and get Dad his meal, but I thought I could make it to Hannah's Inn by eight-thirty. So, I replied that it was fine. I got Dad his burger and hurried back.

"Here, Dad," I said, when I got into the apartment. I handed him the paper bag with his burger and fries inside.

He said, "Thank you," and "Good luck," as I left to jump back into the car.

I sped off and headed to meet Cecilia.

2

At Hannah's Inn, there was a lounge on the side of the building. It had less college kids and was aimed at adults who liked to dance and have a good time. I thought it would be less crowded—that's why I invited Cecilia here. It was a big place with chairs and low tables throughout. It had a jukebox and there were different strobe lights all along the ceiling. The bar was long—all the way down the side of the lounge—and there were two bartenders on staff. It was a good place to sit and chat.

I walked in and looked around for Cecilia, wondering if she was already there. My eyes jumped from table to table, until, finally, I saw her towards the corner of the bar, sitting and writing in her journal just like at the coffee shop. It was so dark in here I don't know how she could see her writing. I headed towards her.

"Hey," I said, once I reached her. She didn't hear me. It was too loud. Instead, I sat down and smiled. She looked up at me and returned the smile.

"Hey!" she said. "You made it!"

"Of course," I replied. I waited a moment then looked down at her journal. "May I ask what you're writing?"

She laughed. "You'll think it's silly," she said.

"No. No, I won't. Go ahead. Tell me!"

"I'm writing a book. These are my ideas and kind of a story plot," she replied. "See. It's silly."

"Not at all," I said. "I'd love to read it when it's finished. Really. That's cool!" I was being genuine. Not only was she beautiful, but she was intelligent. I liked that. It was refreshing.

"How did you know about this place?" she asked me.

I replied, "You've never been here before? It's great. Isn't it?"

"I like it," she said, "But I had no idea it existed until tonight."

Her smile was contagious. Every time she looked at me, I returned the smile back at her.

"It's a nice place to have a drink," I said. "Not too many people come in here. It's really easy-going. I like it." I nodded. "Can I get you a drink, Cecilia?"

"Yes," she replied. "I'll take a rum and Coke."

"That's what I drink. I'll get us two. Hold on. Stay here!" I got up from my seat and made my way to the bar. The bartender saw me and hurried over.

"What can I get ya?" she said.

"Two rum and Cokes please!" I had to yell over the music. It was god-awful pop music—today's top 40—but in this situation, I didn't mind; I enjoyed being here with Cecilia, no matter how terrible the music was.

The bartender gave me a thumbs up then began working on our drinks. I turned around and leaned back on the bar. I peered around the room. There was a couple over near the jukebox who were very touchy and laughing at whatever they were talking about, there were three people—middle-aged—who seemed like old friends near the dartboards, and lastly, down the bar seated, was an older gentleman holding his glass and occasionally taking a sip—he might have been drinking straight whiskey.

"Two rum and Cokes," the bartender said, as she scooted them towards me on top of the bar. I paid and hurried back to Cecilia.

"Here you go," I told my date, as I sat her drink in front of her on the paper napkin.

"Thank you," she replied, with a smile.

She took hold of her glass and began to stir the drink with the short, black straw. Her nails were long, hair a vibrant red, and she had tattoos all up and down both arms. Her nose was pierced in three different places. Although I had a few tattoos myself, I wasn't as *alternative* as her. But I hoped she still liked me, nonetheless.

"Thank you for the drink," she said to me. She smiled and lifted it to her lips.

I took a swig. "You're welcome," I replied. "So, what do you do for work, Cecilia?" I asked her. I was sincerely intrigued.

"Oh, nothing special—I work at a bank," she said. "It's very boring and long hours. You wouldn't want to hear about it. I'll put you to sleep." She laughed.

"No, no," I said, "I want to hear about it. Really. Go on."

"I'm a teller," she replied. "I've been there about three years now. I used to work at a restaurant. But then I jumped to the bank when I got the opportunity. Just wanted a change of pace."

"Really? That's what I do—restaurants—I cook," I said. "I know what you mean though. I wish I could change it up and do something else sometimes, but I don't have any other skills. Plus, I don't get paid too badly, either. It's not horrible. It could be worse."

"Exactly," she said. "I did it for several years. I got burnt out, I guess. I just couldn't stand making burgers anymore."

"Oh, tell me about it. I get burnt out every day," I said, then chuckled. "I'm not sure if I enjoy it anymore like I used to. It's not like when I was twenty-one and really getting after the tickets. I kind of find myself just going through the motions and just trying to stay afloat with bills and such." I paused, then said, "My father stays with me. He has COPD and wears an oxygen mask. He recently lost his insurance—well, they plan to discontinue it—and, frankly, I'm a little worried about what I'm going to do to keep my dad alive and going. He takes a variety of medicine that he absolutely needs so I'm trying to figure this all out before the insurance is canceled. It's very frustrating, terrifying, and unnerving. It's all up to me and I don't know what to do, Cecilia."

She looked down at her drink. Then, with a smile, placed her hand on the back of my hand. "It'll be okay, Sam," she said. "You will figure it all out. If it's meant to be, it'll be. I know there's a way."

I smiled back. Her touch was soft on my hand. It felt nice.

"You want to get out of here?" she asked.

"Where do you want to go?"

"Follow me!" she said, then stood up.

We made our way out of the lounge and into the parking lot.

"Just follow me," she said, then laughed.

I got into my car and drove behind her. I had no idea where she was taking me.

3

After fifteen minutes of following close behind her while she was driving, we pulled up to the go-kart racetrack on the edge of town. It was an arcade, a café, and raceway.

No way.

I got out of my car.

She walked up. "Yeah? Wanna race?" she asked.

"You're going down," I said.

She took me by the hand, and we went into the lobby area to get tickets. She paid for the both of us and led me to the outside racetrack. We got in line. It wasn't very long considering it was almost ten o'clock at night.

"You're wild," I said, as I looked into her deep eyes.

She was perfect. This was unexpected.

"Just trying to live my best life," she replied. "I'm glad you didn't say no."

She nudged my arm with her fist.

"Who doesn't love go-karts?"

After the first race was finished, it was our turn to enter the gate and pick a kart. We walked through the fence and found ourselves a couple of karts. I picked the blue one, and she picked out a yellow one.

I sat down inside of it and strapped myself in. I looked over at her and she winked at me with a smile. The racetrack associate came over and tugged on my seatbelt to make sure it was fastened properly.

"All ready?" the associate yelled out.

He closed the gate and stood back.

There was a stop light in front of us with the red signal on—yellow and green were dim.

"Let's go!" he hollered, then the green light flashed.

I hit the gas pedal.

Cecilia was in front of me, and she took off first. A few people went, then it was my turn to go. We all left the garage.

I quickly caught up to Cecilia.

We were going around a curve and she was on my left. I was on the inside and I looked over at her with a grin. She yelled out something inaudible, and I howled back. I began to pass her until a young man cut me off.

"Hey!" I yelled. Cecilia passed me too. "Damn it!"

I wasn't last because there were two teenage girls that were behind me. But I kept on.

I was right behind Cecilia. She looked back at me and made a face that looked like she just ate something sour and stuck out her tongue at me. I shook my fist in the air at her.

"I'm gonna get you!" I screamed.

I started to gain on her and lessen the distance between our karts. By this time, we had gone around the track twice, and it was only three laps allowed. On the third lap, I still didn't pass her, and it was time to pull back into the garage. The yellow light was flashing on and off.

Damn. She won.

She parked, and soon after, so did I.

Cecilia got up and out of her kart and I did the same.

"Wasn't that great?" she asked, walking up to me.

"For sure!"

"Well, it's getting late, Sam, and I have work tomorrow," she said to me. "We should probably head out."

I nodded and followed her towards the lobby.

"I had fun though," she said.

"So did I," I replied.

I walked her out and to her car.

She stopped before getting into her car and turned around to look at me.

"Let's do this again," she said, and smiled. She turned back to her car and got in. I stood and watched her put on her seatbelt. When she started to drive off, I walked away to my car.

It was a pleasant night and more than I could have ever asked for. I had fun and she was great. I was happy. I hadn't been happy in a very long time.

11

Chapter 11

1

I pulled up to my apartment complex and sat in the car for a moment.

Should I text her 'Goodnight'?

I forgot to tell her when we left the go-kart racetrack.

No, Sam. Leave it alone.

I was holding my phone and looking down at it.

Tell her 'Good morning' instead. Perfect.

I got out of my car and walked up to my apartment.

It was about eleven o'clock when I entered through the front door, and all was quiet. The television was on, but it was at a low volume.

"Dad," I whispered into the living room. "I'm home."

He should have been on the couch.

Maybe he's in his room.

I started to walk to find him. I almost ran him over before I saw him on the ground lying face down.

"Dad!" I yelled.

I dropped to my knees by his side and turned him over. His weight was heavy, but I managed to get him to his back.

"Dad," I kept on yelling.

He seemed lifeless. I didn't know how long he had been on the floor like this.

"Dad, wake up!"

I smacked the side of his face to try to make him conscious.

He wasn't wearing his oxygen mask. I put my ear to his mouth. He was breathing, but it was light.

"Thank, God!"

I took out my cell phone and dialed 9-1-1 in a hurry.

"9-1-1. What's your emergency?"

"My dad—he's unconscious. I found him on the floor. I don't know what happened." I was frantic.

"Calm down," the lady-operator told me.

After a moment on the phone with her, she told me shew was sending an ambulance over.

I put my phone on the floor.

"Dad," I said, as I held him and started to cry. "Dad, come back to me. Please come back."

I sat on the ground holding my father. It seemed like an eternity. He lay in my arms, helpless like a small child. I didn't know what to do so I held him close until help arrived. I had told the operator where I lived and which apartment. I waited until the paramedics got here. It didn't seem fast enough, however.

2

Finally, the EMTs showed up at our door. They hurried in and laid down their bags next to my dad. They were saying medical terms and things that I had no clue about. I just stood there, a few feet away, as they tried to get my dad to say something to them.

"Mr. Williams, can you hear me?" one of them asked my dad, who was still on the floor.

It was almost unbearable to watch. My hands were tied, and I felt useless in this moment.

"Mr. Williams," the other one said, "I'm an EMT, and I'm here to help you. Can you squeeze my hand if you can hear me?"

I wasn't sure if my dad squeezed or not. He just appeared to be laying dead on the floor. He wasn't moving, but I knew he was breathing. After a moment, they put him on a gurney and moved him downstairs and into the ambulance. I followed close, but I made sure not to get in the way. They got him inside the ambulance which had it's lights flashing. There was a small crowd gathered now on the sidewalk. I looked and couldn't believe how the people were just gawking. The EMT shut the doors of the ambulance truck and I headed for my car. I wanted to meet my dad at the hospital. I didn't want him to be alone.

I walked to my car looking back over my shoulder every so often and then the ambulance pulled away. I got in and started up the engine.

"Fuck!" I screamed, and slammed my hands on the wheel.

I pulled out of my parking space and got onto the main road to go to the hospital.

3

I pulled up to the hospital. From where I was, I could see the two EMT take out my father out of the ambulance.

Dad, please be okay.

I sat for a moment holding back tears. I didn't want anyone to see me cry. I wasn't ashamed. I just didn't want pity. I had enough of that during my 20s being schizophrenic and people saying, "Aw, I'm sorry that has happened to you." I didn't want it. Not then, and not now.

I left the car and headed for the lobby of the hospital. A tall, robust woman sat at the front desk. She was wearing light blue scrubs and had her hair up tight.

"Excuse me," I said to her, trying to grab her attention away from the computer monitor she was looking at.

She finished typing, then looked up at me. "Yes?" she asked.

"My father just came in. I need to know where they took him. Please."

"Name?"

"Williams. Simon Aaron Williams," I replied.

She looked back at her computer monitor, typed, used the

mouse to scroll, and she looked back up. "You'll have to wait in the lobby. They have taken your father up to the ER. He's being looked at right now, and until further notice, we can't let you in to see him."

I sighed. "Thank you." I pushed myself away from the front desk and headed for the waiting room. I took a seat.

After a moment of just staring at the floor, I pulled out my phone and scrolled through my contacts. I found "Marcus Williams", my brother.

I hadn't seen Marcus since mom had passed three years ago. He didn't take the cancer news very well, and after she died, he moved to New York State—I'm guessing to get away from the tragedy and everything that went with it. I wish I could have run away too, some times. But I had dad to think about. I wasn't selfish like my older brother. I had responsibilities at home. Marcus was supposed to stay, man-up, and help me, but instead, he fled. I hated him for it. He just left me with a pile of shit to deal with.

We had been close when growing up. Any trouble he would get into, I was sure to be by his side. I loved my brother, until mom got sick. Then everything got complicated—chemotherapy costs, doctor's visits, and finally, funeral arrangements. It was chaos at that time years ago. But I could deal, and Marcus couldn't. I didn't push him away— no one told him to leave besides himself.

I looked down at my phone and achingly wanted to call my brother. I needed to. I wanted to tell him that something had happened to dad and I was sitting here alone at the hospital. The same hospital mom was in and out of for months during her chemotherapy. The same hospital that the doctor's told her that she had six months to a year to live. The same hospital where we all watched her take her final breath.

I didn't know what happened to dad. I replayed the moment back in my head over and over again. I walked in, it was dark, TV on, and dad on the floor not moving an inch.

What happened?

By this time, it was well passed midnight, and I was in the waiting area falling asleep on one of the uncomfortable chairs after waiting for an hour or two. I wondered if dad was okay.

I never called Marcus. I sat up in the chair and yawned. I stretched my arms and stood up.

I should go and ask about dad.

I headed up to the front desk. By this time, I guess it had been shift-change because now there was a pretty, young woman up front.

"Hi," I said, as I approached her. "I wanted to see what the status was on my father. His name is Simon Williams."

She looked through her computer. "I'll have a doctor come down and speak with you, sir. Just wait a moment."

"Great! More waiting."

I went back to my seat.

After a few minutes, a tall man in a white coat approached me.

"Hi," he said. "Are you Mr. Williams's son?"

"Yes, doctor. What happened to my dad? Will he be all right?"

"He'll be fine," he replied. "He suffered a heart attack. It was pretty minor, but we want him here to observe and to make sure he'll be okay. You can go see him in the morning. He's in room 207, upstairs. I suggest you go home and get rest too. Come back tomorrow. Visiting hours start at 8 am." He walked away.

"A heart attack?" I said to myself. "Jesus."

I left the lobby and was perplexed.

"Where did it come from?" I asked myself, as I got into my car.

I sat down and leaned back in the seat. I sat for a moment staring out the window.

Fuck, dad. I'm sorry.

Tears began to stroll down my face.

"I know you'll be okay," I said, aloud. "You're a fighter. You are now, and you were when mom was here and sick. You'll make it."

I started up the engine, and said, "I'll see you in the morning, dad. I'll be back. I promise."

4

As I lay in bed, I watched the sunlight pour into my room slow like a slithering snake reaching for the corners of my room and killing the darkness a minute at a time. I lay there, thinking about dad and Marcus. Even if I told my brother that dad had a heart attack, would he even care? I wanted dad to be okay.

Selfishly I thought about how I would pay for everything—even the overnight stay at the hospital. We can't afford this. Not now.

I was in a bind and I didn't have many options. I sat up in bed and grabbed my phone off of the nightstand. I scrolled through the contacts in my phone and pulled up Marcus's number.

"I really don't want to talk to you," I said aloud. "But this family needs you."

I pressed the *dial* button and put the phone up to my ear. It rang, and rang. After a moment, there was still no answer.

"Fuck you," I muttered, then put the phone back on the table next to me.

I slouched down into my bed and rest my head on the wall.

"You've never been much of a brother anyway. Mom died, now dad is sick. I need you. But you're never there," I said to myself.

The phone rang.

I got the sensation that it was Marcus calling back. I peered over at the screen and it just read, "SPAM."

"Right," I said. "Figures."

I lay my head back down and closed my eyes.

5

My alarm went off on my phone and I woke up. I had work this morning at the Open House restaurant. I intended to see dad after my shift. I didn't want to call out. I was a good employee. I knew dad would be okay. I decided to get dressed and go into my job. I could visit after four o'clock today.

Out the door and down the stairs of the apartment complex, I went.

Before I could get to my car, my phone started to ring. I pulled it from my pants pocket. On the screen it read "Marcus brother". I was shocked that he was returning my call. I stopped in my tracks on the sidewalk. I hesitated, but eventually answered.

"Hello?"

Marcus said, "Hey, Sam. It's me."

"Yeah. I know. Listen—dad is sick."

Silence.

I continued, "He had a heart attack last night. The doctor said it was minor. I could really use your help here, Marcus." I figured my brother would brush me off. He would weasel his way out of coming down with some kind of excuse. I knew him. I grew up with him. I knew what kind of man he was. Especially after mom died.

"I'll be there," Marcus said, to my surprise. "It'll take me a day or two, but I'll find a flight down."

Now I was the silent one. I didn't know how to respond. My brother wasn't such a selfish asshole after all.

"Are you there, Sam?"

"Yes," I replied quickly. "I—I'm here, man. Yeah, the sooner the better, Marcus. We need you. Dad needs you."

In the middle of the conversation, I got a notification for a text message. I moved the phone away from my face and looked at the screen. It was from Cecilia.

"I had a great time last night. Hope you did too!"

If she only knew.

"Sam. Sam?" I could hear my brother calling for me.

"I'm here," I replied.

"I'll be down. I'll keep in touch."

The phone call ended.

I placed the phone back into my pocket and got into my car. The windows were up. It was quiet. But I felt a sense of relief knowing that Marcus would be down in a day or two from upstate New York. I needed someone to lean on right now. I felt overwhelmed before he called back. I felt like I was about to fall apart. Now, I felt a little easier. I would see dad after work and I hoped he was doing fine—maybe even awake by now enjoying bad hospital breakfast.

It was seven-thirty, and I was due at the restaurant for opening and prep. I started my car's engine and pulled out of my usual space. Then, I headed to work with a sense that everything might be okay after   all.

12

Chapter 12

1

I pulled up to the Open House Bar and Grill. I got out and headed for the door. I had a few minutes until I had to clock in so, once inside, I dug out my phone and opened the text messages between Cecilia and myself.

"I had a great time too," I wrote, and then sent it off.

I hope she didn't think I was ignoring her.

I punched into the computer and headed to the back where the kitchen was.

"Hey, Sam," Greg greeted me.

"Sam," Terry said, "How's it going?"

I wasn't sure if I wanted to speak about my dad just yet. But I did. It was hard to get out into words, but I managed to say to Terry, "Dad had heart attack. He's in the hospital right now."

Terry replied, "No shit? What are you doing here? If it were me, I would be there sitting by him."

"I know," I said. "But I didn't want to miss work."

In the years I've been with the Open House, I've missed work twice, and both times were out of my control. I rarely got sick, never took a day to myself. I was dedicated to this place. It was kind of sick when I really thought about it.

"I'm going to see him after my shift," I followed. "He'll be okay."

Greg interjected my conversation with Terry. "Sam, when you have time, I need calamari please."

I nodded.

One of the veteran waitresses named Melissa came to the back.

She said, "Hey. Can one of you grab me a Coke to put in the front?"

I suppose they were out in the fountain. I offered to grab the pack and haul it up. I just wanted to keep myself busy with work until I could get to the hospital later.

2

The lunch rush was its usual self. Tickets printing and coming in, fries flying in the air, Greg whipping up burgers— it was always intense. Most of our business was from the refinery workers who were out on lunch. Them, and construction workers, and other tradesmen. It was guaranteed that they would show up at eleven o'clock until about one or two o'clock.

I hurried to put the fries in their respective baskets with a piece of deli paper underneath. It served as a cradle to hold the fries and look neat in the miniature baskets. Very pleasant. If it were a burger with queso cheese on top, the burger and fries went straight onto a plate. A little messy, but it was a popular dish amongst those tradesmen who were looking for a hearty meal for lunch.

"Where's my double-meat burger?" Terry yelled.

I looked over at Greg. He was placing cheese on both of the patties.

"One minute," I replied. I had to be loud enough to be audible over the vent-hoods.

Greg handed me the patties on buns. I put the fries next to the burger on the wooden paddle-plate and handed it to Terry.

"Thank you," he said, sarcastically.

3

After the lunch rush, I went for a smoke. I stood outside the building in the back and took a few drags. I couldn't help but think of my father. I hoped he would be okay. His health was already not that great, and a heart attack was just what we needed now. First, his insurance was canceled, and now this. I didn't know what to do about all the bills. I would just have to keep working my two jobs. I couldn't take on a third. It would be too much for me. My anxiety and schizophrenia wouldn't allow it. My doctor told me to maintain a healthy diet and get good rest at night. I was already pushing it. I drew out a pill bottle from my pocket; it was my anxiety medicine. I opened the top and spilled out one pill into the palm of my hand. I tossed it into my mouth, grabbed my drink, and swallowed it down.

Jesus, I hope everything works out.

My smoke was almost done and I had to get back inside to finish up prep before I left for the day. I tossed the cigarette and went back inside.

"Sam," Greg called to me as I entered the kitchen.

I walked up to him.

"Listen," he said, "Terry told me about your dad. It's important. I want you to go ahead and clock out, go see him, and make sure he's doing all right."

"But— "

"I lost my parents a few years back," he said. "You need to check on your dad, Sam."

"Okay," I replied. "Anything I need to do before I go?"

"No," he said. "Clock out."

I walked away and headed for the computer up front.

Greg wanted me to see my dad. I understood that. But, there was a part of me that didn't want to confront all of this. I had talked to my brother earlier that morning. I just wanted him here. It would help— it would help a lot. Coping was not easy.

I clocked out and headed out the door to my car.

I got in and pulled out my phone. I hadn't sent Cecilia a text in a while. It sounded like she had fun last. I did too.

"How's your day?" I wrote.

I pressed the send button.

I leaned back in my seat and exhaled a long breath. I was overwhelmed and I was in a corner.

Dad, I hope you're okay. I know this isn't your fault, but there's only so much I can take and do for you.

I picked my head up, put the keys in the ignition, and started the engine. I pulled away from the parking lot and got onto the highway.

4

I was parked outside of the hospital and sitting in my car.

My phone vibrated. I pulled it out and looked at the screen. Cecilia had replied by the time I got here.

"My day is good! How about yourself?"

Did I want to tell her about dad. Would that make her uneasy?

I didn't know what to write back at the moment, so I simply placed the phone back in my pocket.

My mind went to my older brother, Marcus. He said he would be here in a couple of days. I knew we would fight. He wasn't the same since mom had passed. He had become resentful. He was troubled. He was very close to our mother, and I think when she died, a small piece of him died too. I brushed off the thought and hopped out of my car one foot at a time.

It was about two-thirty and the sun was beaming down brightly. I could feel the heat on my shoulders.

I shut my car door. I headed for the front lobby.

As I walked in, the smell burnt my nostrils. It was a putrid, sour smell— like alcohol, or hydrogen peroxide— *something* that smelt terrible and unnatural.

I made my way to the front desk.

"Yes, can I help you?" the desk woman asked me.

"I'm here to see Simon Williams, my father."

I assumed she pulled him up on her computer.

"Go ahead," she said. "Room 207, next floor."

I walked away.

At the elevator, I pushed the button with the arrow pointing up. It was glowing orange. I waited for the elevator to come to the first floor.

Ding ...

The large, steel doors opened wide and let out a crowd of people. Once vacant, I walked inside following an elderly couple and a young mother holding her infant child.

"Floor?" the elderly man looked at me and asked.

"Second," I replied, with a forced smile.

The doors shut and the elevator took us up. I was headed to room 207.

At the second floor, the large doors opened and I squeezed past the young woman and her child. "Excuse me," I said as I exited.

I walked down the hall. The tile was white, the walls were white, and it seemed everything else was too, except for the steel beds and trays along the walls. I found room 207 and entered.

My dad was propped up in bed. He saw me right away.

"Sam!" he said, with a big smile.

I immediately walked up to him and grabbed him tight. I hugged him like I hadn't seen him in years.

"I'm sorry, dad," I said.

"Boy, what are you sorry for?" He chuckled.

"I should have been there," I said. "I'm sorry I wasn't there."

"Sam, it's not your fault. The doctor's say it was mild. I'm fine, really."

He placed a hand on my back and patted my shoulder.

"The doctor says," my dad continued, "that I can leave in a few days. They want me here for observation, make sure I'm doing good and all. I'll be home in no time, Sam."

Tears started to form around the bottoms of my eyes. I held onto my father. I guess he could here me whimper.

He said, "Don't cry, Sam. I'm fine."

I didn't want to lose my father, too. It was so hard losing my mother. I couldn't bare both of them lost.

I wiped my eyes and got off my father. I stood and smiled. "I'm happy you're okay," I told him. "I need you, old man."

He laughed. "I know you need me. It's why I'm still here— it's my job. Can't quit my *job* so soon, Sam."

At that moment, I thought of Marcus.

Should I tell my dad he would be here in a couple days?

I didn't want to overwhelm my father, so I kept quiet and didn't say a word about Marcus coming. Instead, I pulled up a chair next to my father and kept him company for the next hour. We talked about old times, happy times, my mother, and that boat my dad had when I was a teenager that we never took out into the water— he'd fixed it up for   nothing,   only   to   sell   it   to   a   friend.

13

Chapter 13

1

I was driving home from visiting my dad in the hospital when I felt my phone vibrate. I took it out and glanced at the screen. It was Cecilia. She asked how everything was and reiterated how nice of a time she had last night. I didn't want her to think I thought different, so I made it a point to text her as soon as I pulled into the apartment complex. I put the phone back and kept on my way home.

By this time, as I pulled into my space at the complex, it was nearing six o'clock. I parked the car and drew out my phone, pulled up my conversation with Cecilia, and wrote to her.

I said, *"Hey, long day. But it's nice to hear from you. I'm glad you had fun also! What are you up to this evening?"*

I didn't tell her about dad. I didn't want to get so personal too soon. I wasn't sure how she would respond, so I kept it casual.

I sat there and waited for a reply. A few minutes passed, then my phone vibrated. I had it face-down on my leg. I turned it over. On the screen I could see what she wrote back.

"I'm not doing a thing," she said. *"Do you have any plans?"*

I figured she was fishing.

Should I ask her out to dinner? Was it too soon? It's only been a day. I should let a cooler head take over. No need to rush.

I replied, *"Not really. Maybe catch a bite."*

I couldn't help myself though.

I then wrote, *"Do you want to join me?"*

I could use a change of pace. Being at the hospital made me uneasy and seeing dad wired up to all those machines put me on edge. I needed something different.

I waited patiently as I figured she was debating on her answer. After a moment, I decided to get out of the car and head upstairs. I locked the car behind me and climbed up to the second floor where our apartment was. I went in and threw my keys on the bar.

I looked at my phone. No reply yet.

That's okay. Maybe she really was interested? Maybe she did have a bad time?

As I kicked off my shoes and headed to lay on my bed, my phone went off. I was excited. This time it was *just* Terry.

Damn it, Terry.

He wrote, *"How is your dad? Just checking in, bud."*

I threw my phone on the bed before I laid down. I took off my shirt and threw it in the hamper.

It went off again.

"Fuck, Terry," I muttered, annoyed.

Cecilia's name was at the top of my notifications with a reply.

Oh.

"I would like to go out with you again, Sam," she replied. *"When and where?"*

"Yeah!" I hollered. I imagined the downstairs neighbors heard that yell.

Concentrate, you fool!

I calmed myself down. Breathe. I took the phone into my hands and carefully thought of what to say next.

"How about burgers uptown in an hour?"

I sent it.

An hour would give me enough time to wash up and put on fresh clothes.

"I need some of that smell-good stuff," I said.

She responded, *"Sounds great! I'll be ready."*

Awesome!

I grabbed some nice clothes and headed for the bathroom to shower.

2

I pulled up to the little burger joint.

"Did you make it okay?" I asked Cecilia, as I got out of the car and closed the door behind me.

She must have arrived a bit earlier. She was standing on the sidewalk waiting for me.

"Yeah," she replied. "I know this place. My dad and I used to come here when I was little before my parents divorced. It was our family *thing.*"

I wasn't sure how to reply. I wanted to say, "That's sweet," because of the memory, but, then again, it had to do with divorce, so I didn't say anything at all. I didn't think Cecilia minded my lack of response. She seemed easy-going and cool. I didn't feel judged by her at all.

I stepped onto the sidewalk and stood next to her.

"Chilly tonight," I said, as I crossed my arms. A cool-front had blown in as I was getting ready at home. It had to have been in the sixties. There was a *bite* to the night air.

"Yes, it feels amazing," she replied.

She was smart. She had brought a soft coat. I, on the other hand, wore a short-sleeved tee shirt.

"You're cold," she said, with a smile. She took a step towards me and wrapped her arms around my waist. She looked up at me. "Better?"

I simply smiled.

"Let's go inside," she said, and drew back.

I followed her into the burger restaurant.

It was loud. They were playing country music. The waitresses were walking fast back and forth throughout the dining area. I could hear the cooks yelling at each other in the kitchen.

"Where do you want to sit?" I hollered, hoping she heard me as I kept up behind her. But she didn't acknowledge me, so I guess she hadn't heard me. We reached a table and she took a seat.

"Is this okay?" she asked me.

"Great," I replied, and sat down.

She took off her coat and placed it onto the back of her seat. I still had my arms crossed. It might have been cooler in the restaurant than it was outside.

"Maybe we can ask them to raise the temperature?" she said.

I replied, "No, no, it's fine. I'll be all right."

I was being stubborn. I was, in fact, freezing my ass off.

I grabbed the menus that were on the inside of the table next to the wall and handed one to Cecilia, so she could look through it.

"What do you usually get here?" I asked her.

"I don't know. I haven't been here in a year or two. I don't have a favorite."

I replied, "The bacon cheese burgers are pretty good."

She smiled, then looked down at the menu.

The waitress came walking up to the table, and asked, "What can I start you two off with to drink?"

I looked at Cecilia and gestured that she should answer first.

She replied, "I'll just have a Coke."

I looked up at the waitress. "Yeah, me too."

"Great,"she said, and walked away.

"I did hope you had a good time last night," I blurted to Cecilia.

She smiled. "I did. Did you?"

"Oh, yes," I replied, thrilled. "I had a great time!"

"I wasn't sure," she said, with a grin. "Since I beat you and all at the karts." She chuckled.

I said, "Hey, I would have won if it weren't for those kids getting in my way." I joined in on the laughter. I put down my menu, and looked into Cecilia's eyes. "Can I tell you something?"

"Sure," she replied.

"I like you," I told her. "Like ... I'm glad I ran into your car."

She laughed.

"I want to tell you something about myself," I said.

Normally, I wasn't so forward, but I felt like Cecilia wouldn't judge me for my mental health, so I told her I had been diagnosed *Bipolar schizo-effective*.

"It's not something I share too often," I said. "I keep it pretty private. Only my family really knows. Dad went through a lot when I was first diagnosed."

"Thank you for telling me," she said. "It's okay."

I was looking down at the table avoiding eye-contact. She reached over and put her hand on mine.

"You're fine," she reassured me.

I smiled.

The waitress came back with our drinks and sat them down onto the table. She asked us, "Are you guys ready to order?"

We hadn't even looked at the menus. We had just been talking. I was enjoying Cecilia's company so much that I forgot to pick a burger.

"I know what I want," Cecilia said, looking at me.

"I'll take the bacon cheese burger with mayo," I told the waitress.

"Same," Cecilia said.

I looked at her. She had a grin on her face. She was being slick. I could tell. I almost laughed.

"Awesome, guys! Thank you," the waitress said, then headed off to the kitchen to turn in our order.

Cecilia's hand was still on top of mine. I looked at it. She looked down at our hands, too.

"Sorry," she said, laughed, and drew her hand back.

"It's fine. It's *nice*," I told her. "I haven't felt something in a very long time. I'm not good at these things."

"What do you mean?" she asked.

I replied, "I'm not a very good *boyfriend*."

She looked puzzled. "I'm sure you are, Sam. You just haven't met the right person to appreciate everything that you have to offer and give."

"Maybe," I said.

I never thought of myself as boyfriend-material. There was one relationship I thought *special* back in 2018, but that ended, too, just like all the others. Honestly, I had really sewn my oats in my twenties. I was an avid "dating-app enthusiast", a real "serial meet-n-greet, then lay them down" kind of guy. I wasn't proud of that fact, but it's what I did and I would own up to it if anyone had ever asked. But no one cared about my past. Maybe Terry might ask over a couple of beers, but he was about the only one.

Truth was— Cecilia was right. I put my faith in terrible women that I could never fully open up to. I was always guarded. After being cheated on for the first time years ago, I had never been the same. I always had the inkling that my *then* girlfriends at the time were cheating— talking to someone behind my back, or seeing someone when I wasn't around. *Shit.* Just a few years ago, I had one girlfriend that was exceptionally younger and she *was* cheating. I knew because one night, after learning her pass-code to her phone, I looked through her messages to see if I was right or not. Sure enough, I found evidence that she was unfaithful. We fell apart soon after that, and I guess the hurt got to me so bad. I ended up in the mental hospitals and couldn't quite handle reality for the better part of 2021. It wasn't until that Fall that I grasped onto myself again and put my train back on its' tracks, so to speak.

3

Our burgers arrived in about fifteen minutes. I was glad. Cecilia and I were talking about relationships, and it was tiring. I didn't like to look back. But to keep the conversation going, I mentioned some bad relationships, and some successful ones. They still ended, but I was pretty happy and content in a few of those. Every woman I had ever dated or slept with wasn't all bad. Each was unique. I was looking for something in my twenties. I don't think I ever found it, so I ended up alone, and worked full-time. Recently, I was focusing on my health and taking care of my father. I hadn't the need to go on dates. But Cecilia was an exception and someone I wanted to get to know. I felt I was ready to try again. I hope Cecilia would be the one.

"Salt?" I said, as I raised the shaker.

She replied, " No. Thank you."

I took a sip of Coke and bit into my cheese burger with bacon.

4

"So, are you from here, Cecilia?" I asked.

"Yes. Always from this area. I was born in Corpus. What about you?"

I replied, "I was actually born in Dallas. My parents moved back down her when I was about three years old."

"What do your parents do?" she asked.

I put down my burger.

"I'm sorry," she said. "I said something wrong, didn't I?"

"No. It's fine. My mother died three years ago. The cancer took her."

I guess it was time to confess about dad.

"And my dad— he's actually in the hospital right now."

"Oh, no," her eyes grew wide. "Is he okay?"

"You know last night?" I said. "He had a heart attack. I found him after our date."

"Jesus," she exclaimed.

"You probably think bad of me now, right? My dad's in the hospital and I'm here with you instead of him. I'm a terrible son."

She put her hand once again on mine, and said, "I don't think bad of you, Sam. There's only so much you can do. How is he?"

I took another sip of my coke, and said, "He's good now. I think he's in good spirits. I saw him earlier— after work— and he seemed lively. I think it just scared me more than anything. My dad's always been my hero and closest friend. I don't know what I would do if I lost him. I've already lost my mom, and she was my everything, too."

Cecilia gave me a look of compassion. I could tell she wanted to console me. Her eyes glowed beneath the diner's overhead lights and her red hair looked like fire. The smile she offered was enthralling. Her skin, milky. I felt her kindness and without words, I knew she was being sincere in her concern.

5

After dinner, we decided to go for a walk to the park down the street. Her hand was in mine as we walked down the sidewalk together.

"You mentioned your parents were divorced," I said to Cecilia.

She looked up at me, smiled, and then looked forward. She said, "Yes. My dad found out that my mom had been having an affair. She apparently had been secretly talking to another man for some time without him knowing. He didn't catch them in bed or anything. He followed her one day. She left work and he stayed behind her in his truck. When she got to where she was going, got out, and hugged this man, my dad knew in that moment what was going on."

"I'm sorry," I said. I squeezed her hand.

"It's okay. They're happier now separate. I still see my mom. She moved up North, and my dad is still local— I see *him* all the time. But there's one thing I learned though: I hated cheating."

I nodded.

She asked me, "Have you ever cheated on someone?"

"No, actually," I replied. "I always told myself, if I wanted someone new or different that I would break up with the person I was with to pursue the other."

"Good policy," she replied.

"I think so," I said, and grinned.

She laughed, then said, "It is a nice night for walk. Not hot like it usually is, right?"

"Exactly," I replied.

I was enjoying holding her hand. It felt comfortable and right. I thought maybe this could really turn into something; it was possible to grow a relationship with Cecilia.

"I wish we could go see your dad," she said.

I was surprised, but said, "I think it's late for visiting hours. But that's sweet of you."

"Yeah. I would like to meet him."

"I bet he'd like you," I replied.

"I hope so. But I am kind of likable."

She shoved my shoulder. She was being flirtatious and I liked that. I squeezed her hand. It was small and fit perfectly in mine. Although she was almost as tall as me, her hands were small.

As we made our way down to the park, we talked more about family and our on-going lives. She told me she had family up in Arkansas and Oklahoma— where her mom moved to, I learned— and that they visit every now and again. I learned she had three sisters. They were all older by a lot. She was the youngest. The age gap was about seven years from her to the second youngest; the oldest was in her fifties. I told her I had a brother.

"His name is Marcus," I said, as we entered the park and made our way onto the sidewalk that went all the way around. "He will actually be here in two days— well, that's what he claims."

"What do you mean by that?"

I said, "After our mom died, he vanished to up-state New York. No warnings— he just packed and left. I don't know why to this day. I don't know if it was the pain of her loss, or he didn't want to deal with dad, or what really happened. But it annoys me that he took off like that."

"I'm sorry," Cecilia said. "Must be hard taking care of your dad all by yourself."

"His insurance was canceled recently also. Now, it's even more difficult, and I've had to pick up a second job. I'm working both tomorrow. It makes for very long days— I leave a little after sunrise and get home way after dark."

"Sounds tiring," she said. "There's no alternatives for the insurance?"

"I'm hoping Marcus, my older brother, *will* come down and offer help. I don't need his money, but it would be easier having him here when dad gets out of the hospital."

She nodded and looked around. She then took my arm into both of hers and held onto it tight. We walked closely like this for a bit longer. I realized it was getting late and I had work in the morning.

"I'll have to walk you back," I told her. "It's late."

"I know," she replied.

She looked up at me and smiled. Her eyes were shaped like almonds, and the hazel glowed beneath the lamp posts. I put my hands on her sides and leaned in. I put my lips on hers and she pressed against me. I guess this was happiness.

14

Chapter 14

1

The next morning, I lifted myself out of bed. The phone read, "6:30 am," and it was time to get the day started. I was at odds with my feelings—I was hurt that dad was in the hospital, but I was happy that Cecilia kissed me last night. I didn't know what to feel, so I got dressed and headed out the door to begin the morning at the Open House Bar and Grill.

I had to work both jobs today, and as I entered the Open House, I immediately knew it was going to be a very long, and drawn out day.

"Hey, Sam," Terry said to me, as I entered the kitchen. "How's your dad?"

I looked at him, and said, "He's okay, I guess. The doctors want to keep him a few days for observation— make sure he'll be all right and everything. The doctor said it was minor. But dad's health isn't so great, so I'm still worried."

"Damn," Terry muttered. "I'm sure he'll be fine, Sam. You're dad is a strong guy. He's gotten through worse, I'd imagine."

"Yeah, that's true."

"Sam," Greg said, "I need you to make up patties and bag pickles please."

"On it," I replied.

I decided to portion the pickles first, so I got two containers. One was to put the pickles in, and the other was to hold them after I put them in small sandwich bags. I spent the next twenty minutes weighing out pickles to six ounces and placing them neatly in one of the containers. After that was finished, I went and grabbed two large tubes of hamburger meat.

It was about an hour before we were to open. I had time to prep the patties. I unwrapped them, and placed them in a large, stainless-steel mixing bowl. I added mayo and seasoning, then mixed around the meat with my hands. Once the meat was ready, I grabbed the scale and measured a ball of hamburger meat to eight ounces. I placed the ball to the side and kept going until all of the meat was gone from the bowl.

It was ten-thirty and I needed to hurry and finish. I gave the bowl to the dishwasher and grabbed a long pan. I squished and formed each ball of hamburger meat until it was the shape of a hamburger patty, then I placed it into the pan. Eight would make up a layer of patties. Finally, when I mashed all the patties into circles and had them stacked, I wrapped the pan in clear-wrap and labeled it. I put it in the walk-in cooler on the shelf.

I walked back to the kitchen and readied my station with more chicken fried steak portions, chicken tenders, and fish. I was ready for the lunch rush.

2

During the rush, I couldn't help but think of my brother coming into town. I hoped he would be more helpful than a hindrance. Growing up, he was always my salvation and savior. He would bail me out of trouble if I ever needed him. As kids, we often found trouble, but he was always there by my side. As teenagers, he would guide me, and tell me about girls and life outside of Texas. He would tell me, "Sam, there's a bigger world out there for you and me, little brother. You just got to be brave enough to go find it!" I loved my brother, but I did feel abandoned when he left three years ago. I didn't feel *stuck* with our dad. But his leaving didn't help me feel like I had any support-system. I was resentful and I knew that. I knew I would throw it in his face when I saw him tomorrow. I knew I couldn't help but bring up mom and the past. I knew myself—I wanted to say a lot and get under his skin like he got under mine when I really got to thinking about the entire situation. I'm a cook, and supporting myself and our father on my wage—there wasn't exactly a whole lot of money floating around. Now, with dad's insurance canceled and having two jobs—I was becoming exhausted.

I had to work at Mama Vici's later on and I wasn't looking forward to it. As I cooked here, now, at the Open House, I dreaded clocking out, driving to the little Italian restaurant, and clocking in, there, for another six hours. It took up my entire day, and I felt as if I had no time to myself and to relax.

Finally, it was one o'clock and the rush was over and the pace of everything was slowing down.

"Not a bad one today, huh?" Terry said.

"Make sure to clean up your area," Greg said to Terry. "You didn't yesterday before you left and *I* had to hear about it."

"Yeah, yeah," Terry replied. "Sam," he said. "What are you doing after work?"

I replied, "I've got to go to my second job. It's been a killer on me, but I've got to do for it dad. I don't like it much, but I'm doing it."

"Damn. Sounds tough. I couldn't imagine doing that. I commend you, my friend." He walked away.

I grabbed a rag and started wiping down the steel tables in the kitchen.

3

After four o'clock, I left the Open House and headed to Mama Vici's. I was already tired; I thought I might have just enough energy to last the evening. I was ready to sleep.

As I was driving, my phone began to ring. I dug it out of my pocket and looked at the screen. It was my older brother, Marcus. I answered.

"Hello?"

"Hey, it's me. How's dad?"

What do you care?

"He's doing fine. I saw him. He's in good spirits."

"Listen— my flight leaves in the morning. Can you get me from the airport about noon?" Marcus asked.

I said, "Yes. I'll be there."

"Thanks."

I hung up the phone.

Ten minutes later, I arrived at Mama Vici's. I parked and got out. I dragged myself inside and clocked in. For the next couple of hours I did prep and readied for the dinner rush. Mama Vici's wasn't as busy as the Open House. It didn't have the same customer volume or traffic during the dinner service. It was tolerable, since I was tired as could be—I didn't really want it to be busy, I wanted calm and to just get through the night.

After dinner, I stepped out for a cigarette. I took a drag here and there, and thought of my father. I thought of him in the hospital, laying in the bed. I thought of him alone. It was too late for visitation, but I figured Marcus and I couldn't visit tomorrow after he landed—if he wasn't too lagged from the flight.

Another two hours of work, then I was free to go. I clocked out and headed home. I barreled through the front door of my apartment, kicked off my shoes right away, and headed for bed. I took off my shirt and laid down. I was more than tired. I was *drained*. I lay down and closed my eyes. I was content though. I was off from both jobs tomorrow and all I had to do was get Marcus from the airport. I could sleep easily. My eyes grew heavy and I drifted off.

Goodnight, *world.*

15

Chapter 15

1

My alarm went off. I looked over at my nightstand, but there was no phone. I realized it was in my pocket. I took it out and shut off the alarm.

What time is it?

I forgot to turn off my alarm that I set for work every morning, but today, I was off, so it wasn't necessary. I got up.

I'll just go ahead and make coffee. I'm sure I'll need to pick up Marcus after a while.

I made my way to the kitchen, sluggish, and without energy—eyes half open and yawning. I started the coffee pot and leaned against the counter. I drew out my phone to check my texts. I hadn't paid much attention to my phone yesterday evening (I just wanted to finish the night and get home). I had one from Terry.

"Enjoy your day off!"

Cecilia had written me. *"How is everything?"*

Slowly, I wrote back.

"My brother is coming in to town today. I'm not sure of how excited I am about that. We'll go see dad later today. How are you this morning?"

The coffee pot was finished brewing, so I grabbed a mug from the cupboard and poured myself a strong cup of coffee. Little cream for this morning—I had an eventful day ahead of me with Marcus's arrival.

I made my way to the couch, sat down, and sipped on my cup. I turned on the television—it was the news, dad's favorite. Channel 3 always had something to state, whether it be good or bad, they always had a segment going and a story to tell.

2

Later that morning, I got dressed and prepared myself mentally to pick up my older brother. I told myself not to be too hard on him, but immediately reminded myself that he abandoned my dad and I when we needed him most. I was bitter, but it was hard to remain such as time went on. After a while, I didn't care anymore regardless if he had left Texas or not; I just knew that it was dad and me. It's all that mattered. We just had to move forward after mom's passing.

As I stepped out the door, I reminded myself not to give him a hard time. We were all going through the same thing.

Be kind.

But as I drove to the airport thirty minutes away hidden in Corpus Christi, I felt myself getting cold.

I pulled up and saw him waiting out by the parking lot with one rolling-bag and a small bag in his other hand. My brother was tall, dark, and handsome. He just had that allure that women craved, but I resented. I didn't care for him being mysterious. I cared if he was here to help, or be a nuisance. I didn't need more trouble. I needed a helping hand. I wanted to bring dad home as soon as possible and I didn't want Marcus getting in the way. I'll admit—I did need help financially, but that wasn't the sole reason I called him; I needed my older brother. I wanted his support, and maybe, if he had it hidden deep down within himself, he could show love and compassion as well—if not, at least, to dad.

He walked to the car. I popped open the trunk. I didn't bother getting out. We weren't close like we used to be. I waited for him to throw his bags into the back and get in.

"Hey," Marcus said, as he plopped down into the passenger

seat.

"Hey."

"How's your morning?"

If this is your way of saying, "Sorry," then save it.

I pulled away from the curb. I said, "It's going."

Traffic wasn't too bad about this time. And since it was Sunday, there wasn't that many cars on the road that were usually let out for lunch. The weekdays were much worse. The roads would have been filled with refinery and construction workers on lunch. But not today, not on Sunday.

"I was going to go ahead and stop by the hospital," I said.

My brother replied, "Yeah, I don't know. I'm thinking we just go straight to your apartment so I can relax— long flight, you know?"

I immediately was angry. "Really? You don't want to see dad?"

"It's not that," he said. "I'm just tired. I could wind down, take a nap, and then we can see him later this evening. Yeah?"

"No," I said. "We're going to see him now."

"Sam ..." my brother said.

"It's my car, my place, my rules. Why don't you want to see dad? How can you be so *heartless?*"

"I'm not," he replied, becoming defensive. He raised his hands. "I'm just telling you that I'm tired as shit and I could really use some rest."

I paused for a moment. "You're really going to be this selfish, Marcus? I can't fucking believe you. I knew you hadn't changed."

"Wow, Sam. You know— this is hard for me too."

"Oh, yeah, right. Just like mom."

"Hey. Fuck you, man!" He turned and looked out the window.

"No, fuck you, Marcus. You left. You stuck me with all this shit! Why— why would you do that to me? You could have really saved the day three years ago. You know that? But instead, you ran off to fucking New York."

He looked down at his lap. "Sam, it's hard. You don't understand."

"I understand totally. You couldn't hack it after mom, you picked up and left, and barely kept in contact since the funeral. So, again: fuck you!"

The silence killed me. My heart raced. It almost beat out of my chest.

"And we're going to the fucking hospital," I said.

3

Once at the hospital, we got out of the car and headed for the front lobby. Marcus followed a few paces behind me.

I looked back, and said, "Room 207."

We headed for the elevators.

As we stood, Marcus kept looking around. I had bothered him back in the car. The air was thick with tension.

He looked over at me and said, "I'm sorry."

"Yeah," I replied. "It's cool."

"Let's do this for dad."

"I agree. For dad."

"And I'm sorry for leaving after mom, Sam," he added, as the elevator door opened.

We stepped inside and it shut behind us.

"Press the '2' button," I told him, and he did.

"It's not that I intentionally abandoned you guys; I had my reasons," he continued as we went up the the second floor. "I almost didn't know what else to do."

"Look, Marcus, I was mad, but it's whatever now. Let's just go see dad."

"No. I should have stayed."

The elevator door opened.

"207," I said again, as he walked out of the elevator first.

We went around the corner and walked down a hallway.

"It's that one," I pointed to a big door with a steel handle.

He pushed against it and walked in. I followed behind. He saw dad and his eyes swelled up. Dad was asleep.

"Dad," I said, softly. I didn't want to alarm him.

"Let me," Marcus said.

He walked over to our father, took a seat on a chair next to the bed, and placed a hand on our dad's stomach. "Daddy?"

Our father's eyes opened slowly. He said, "Sam."

"No, dad. It's me— Marcus."

"Mark?" dad said, then smiled.

109

I stood and watched.

"Yeah, dad. It's Mark. I'm here, daddy."

My brother stood up and put an arm around our dad.

"I love you," Marcus said. "I'm so sorry." He began to weep.

I decided to leave the room and let them have some privacy. It had been years since they'd seen each other. Outside of the room, I sent a text to Cecilia.

"We're here at the hospital seeing dad. I hope you're doing well."

I leaned against the wall— waiting and hoping that Cecilia would text back soon. After a moment, she replied.

"I'm glad you and your brother are there visiting. It's good for your dad. It's good for you. P.s. I can't wait to see you again. I keep thinking about the kiss we shared."

I smiled.

"Me too. I had a great night with you. I hope to see you again real soon. Let me get dad home first, then maybe we can go out again."

"I'd like that."

"I'll text you when I get home in a while."

"Okay."

Marcus came out of the room. "Where's his doctor? I want to talk to him."

"I can go grab him," I said.

"Yeah, we need to see how long dad has to stay here and what we need to do to care for him once he's back home."

"Yes. Give me a minute and I'll find a nurse."

Marcus put a hand on my shoulder. "I'm glad I'm here," he said.

I simply looked at him for a moment, then turned away to find the nurse's station.

Down the hall, I found a nurse.

"Excuse me," I said. "My father is in room 207. I need to speak to his doctor."

"Name?" she asked.

"Simon Williams."

"Okay. I'll dispatch the doctor. Wait in the room and he'll be there shortly."

"Thank you." I headed back to the room.

Marcus had gone back in. I walked inside and dad was sitting up in his bed.

"Hey, dad," I said.

"Marcus is here," he said, smiling.

"I know, dad. I picked him up from the airport."

"Good," my dad replied. He looked at Marcus. "Tell me, son. What have you been doing all this time while you were away?"

Marcus was sitting in the chair next to our dad's bed. He said, "Finances."

"Interesting," dad said. "Banking can be lucrative."

The doctor entered the room.

"Hey, doctor," Marcus got up out of the seat and shook his hand.

"Hello. I'm doctor Erikson."

My brother didn't hesitate. He asked, "When can our father come home?"

The doctor looked at me then faced my brother. "He can go home tomorrow, but he needs rest. He can't have any stress. Although the heart attack was minor, he still needs to watch himself."

My brother nodded. "We can do that. Right, Sam?"

"Yes," I replied.

"Good," the doctor said. "You can check him out in the morning." He looked to our dad. "Mr. Williams, take it easy from here on out please. I don't want to see you back in here again." He smiled, paused, then turned to leave the room.

After he left, we both sat down to be with my father. We spent the next hour talking and reminiscing about old times.

16

Chapter 16

1

We got back to the apartment a little after seven o'clock. Marcus dragged in his bags. I could tell he was tired.

"You can have dad's room for the night," I said.

"Yeah. Thanks."

He disappeared into our dad's room and shut the door behind him.

I went to my room, flopped down on my bed, and held my phone.

"Hey."

I was hoping Cecilia would write back. After a minute, my phone went off.

"How's your dad?"

"He's well. He was laughing."

"How's your brother?"

"It's weird. I haven't seen him in a very long time. I feel distant, but I also feel like he never left. It's strange. I can't explain it."

"It's okay. I get what you're saying."

"Would you like to walk the park again? Maybe go feed the ducks?"

"I'd like that. When?"

"In an hour. Meet me."
"Okay."

2

Cecilia and I were at the park. It was eight-thirty now and the sun was starting to set. The light on her red hair shined and almost burned my eyes. When she'd look up at me, I felt she was looking *into* me—like she could *read my every thought.* I hadn't felt this in a very long time.

We walked around the park three times before we settled on the bench by the pond.

"Did you bring food for the ducks?" she asked.

"No," I replied. "I forgot, I guess."

She laughed. "It's okay. We can just look."

"Okay," I said. I looked away.

"What's wrong?" she asked.

I looked back at her. "Nothing."

"Oh, come on. Is it your dad?"

"No. I guess—I just haven't felt like this in years. You're the first person in a long time to make me feel *seen.* I can't explain it. I'm sorry."

"Don't be sorry. Yes, I know what you mean. I like you too."

I smiled. I took her hand in mine. "I want to sit here with you forever, Cecilia."

"We can try," she said.

3

It was ten o'clock when I got home.

I walked into my apartment and Marcus was sitting on the couch looking at his phone.

He said, "Hey."

"Hey," I replied. "I'm going to bed."

"Yeah, it is pretty late. Let's get dad around eight. What do you say?"

"We can do that. I'll see you in the morning."

I walked to my room, undressed, and laid down. I thought of Cecilia as I looked up at the ceiling. The fan whirled around slowly. I felt a smile on my face. I'm glad she liked me too. It made me feel on top of the world. I felt a genuine connection with her and I thought us getting to know one another could actually *go somewhere.*

4

I must have dozed off because when I opened my eyes and looked over at my phone, it read, "Six thirty."

Oh, shit.

I slowly climbed out of bed.

Marcus knocked then opened my door. He peaked his head in.

"Get dressed. Let's go get dad."

"Yeah, I said.

I was so groggy almost delirious. The past few days were a blur in my mind.

I put on my shoes. A moment later, I didn't even remember doing that. I stumbled out of my room, one foot after the other, while yawning. A good arm-stretch and eyes half-open.

"Ready?" Marcus asked, jingling my keys in his hand.

I guess he was a morning person. I didn't recall that three years ago before he had left town. We went down to the car and took off.

As I drove the car, there was a thick tension in the air. I could tell Marcus wanted to say something—or a few things. But he remained quiet and looked out the window.

"Just say it," I said, finally, and gripping the wheel tightly. "What—what now, man?"

"I took the week off, Sam," he replied. "I wanted to be here for dad—and you. You two need me, so I'm here."

I was surprised.

He's willing to sacrifice a week's worth of work for me—well, dad— us?

"Okay," I said. It was all I could think of. I drove and wished I hadn't broken the silence.

5

It was a   Monday, and we just pulled up to the hospital. I had trouble finding a space because it was so crowded. I settled for a spot in the back near the dumpsters. Marcus hopped out of the car and I was a snail slowly climbing out of the driver's side until I was standing on the hot pavement. The Texas sun was unforgiving.

"Hot," my brother said.

"Yeah. It's supposed to cool down in a week or two."

"We'll see. I remember these hot days."

"Oh, really?" I was being sarcastic. I didn't think he remembered anything about life here in Texas after three years of being away.

"Let's get him." Marcus slammed the door.

He knew I was being a brat, but he ignored me. He walked up to the hospital and I followed closely behind. The lobby was just about full. There were people waiting to be seen, there were others waiting for nine o'clock for visiting hours to start, and then there were those people that just filled the hospital because they were *lost souls* and had no where else in particular to be, I suppose. We passed all of them and made it to the elevators. My brother pressed the "Up" arrow. We waited, then once the door's opened, we entered.

"I bet he'll be happy to see us," my brother said, with a soft smile.

I told him, "You've got to remember Marcus: He's up there in age *and* he's on oxygen."

"Yeah, but he's still the same old *dad.*"

"After mom passed, he really hasn't been the same, man," I told my brother. "He's not as happy without her. He's different. He hasn't changed, but he's—he's not the *same.*"

We reached the second floor and the doors to the elevator opened.

"Come on," Marcus said.

He stepped out and headed for dad's room.

We walked in to see the nurse dressing dad.

"Hey," he yelled. "My boys!"

"Hey, dad," I said.

"Dad, you look good," Marcus said, with arms spread open. He almost pushed the nurse out of the way and took dad in his arms and gave him a big hug.

"Sir," she said. "I have to finish."

"Yeah, yeah. It can wait. His two boys are here!"

"Marcus ..." I said.

"What?"

"Let the nurse do her job, please."

Marcus backed away and waved the nurse forward, gesturing towards our dad.

"The doc said I'm as healthy as a twenty-one-year-old!" dad said. "He feels like this whole 'heart attack' thing was a fluke. It was just a *little thing.*"

"Well, you still have to take it easy," I said.

"Yeah, dad. No heavy lifting, drinking, smoking, and or women," Marcus said, while laughing.

I looked at him. My brother could be somewhat of an insensitive idiot on the occasion. I remembered that now about him.

"Just gotta get dressed, then we can head out, guys," dad added.

His eyes were wide and he was gleeful.

"Stand, please," the nurse said.

She had put on his socks and shirt. She put his pants on partially up to his calves. Once he was in an upright position, she finished bringing up his jeans to his waist.

"Looking good, old man," Marcus said.

I rolled my eyes.

"One of you need to sign him out on your way through the lobby exit," the nurse said, looking at me.

"I've got it," Marcus said.

"Just a signature," she added, then nodded still looking at me. "Okay," she looked at dad. "You're all set, Mr. Williams."

"His oxygen?" my brother asked.

"They're bringing that now," the nurse replied.

6

We waited in the room for another nurse to bring dad's oxygen tank in and ready him for the journey home.

"Dad, you're going to be fine," Marcus said to him.

Dad was sitting on the edge of the bed and Marcus in the chair beside him. He placed a hand on dad's knee.

"Well, of course," dad replied. "Why wouldn't I be? I'm young,

I'm spry, I'm a million bucks!"

Marcus laughed.

"We'll get home soon," I told my dad.

For some reason, I felt choked up. I held back tears. I was happy— happy that dad was coming home and it wasn't worse than it was. I'm glad I found him as soon as I did.

What if I had stayed out that night?

So many scenarios ran through my head. I was happy now, though. I'm glad it went this way and dad was almost home. Just minutes away from leaving.

A nurse walked in and she strolled in a long silver and green oxygen tank that had two wheels at the bottom of it. She rolled it next to dad and untied the hose and mask. She put it over dad's face and turned the knob on the tank to let the oxygen through the hose.

"Mr. Williams, I hope you have a safe trip home and it was a pleasure," she said. "He's funny and a real gentleman," she said, looking at Marcus. He only smiled at her.

"Thank you," I said.

"You all can go now," she finished. She stood up and saw us out of the room.

We made our way to the elevator slowly. We had to walk at dad's pace. He had a bad back from all the years of being a mechanic and had a slight hunch. He walked with stiff knees and joints that you could almost hear *crack*. The elevator door's opened and we entered.

"I'm happy to be going home, boys," he said to the both of us, as the elevator went down to the first floor.

The doors parted open, and I said, "So are we, dad. We love you."

We checked him out and left the hospital.

It   was   a   scare   I'd   never   forget.

17

Chapter 17

1

We walked into the apartment after slowly getting dad up the stairs of the complex.

"Watch your step," Marcus said to dad.

Dad had a grip on his arm. I turned on the lights.

"Welcome home," I said, and threw down the keys on the counter of the kitchenette.

"I took up in your room last night, dad. I'll get my things, so you can rest."

"Leave them," dad replied. "You can get them later, son."

Marcus nodded and helped dad into his room. I stood and watched. My phone rang.

"Hello?"

It was Greg, from work. "Hey, I need to take tomorrow off. Can you run the flat-top for lunch and watch the kitchen? You'll need the practice anyway when I leave in another week."

"Yeah. No worries," I said.

"Okay. Great!"

He hung up.

I was ready to step in as the main cook for lunch. I had been with the restaurant for a long while. I had previous experience elsewhere—at a few different places actually—but I had never been the primary cook at the Open House Bar and Grill. I was excited, yet nervous. It was a lot of pressure. All the stress would be on my shoulders, but I could handle it. I was sure.

Since dad was going to rest in his room for the remainder of the morning and maybe even into the afternoon, I headed for my room. I wanted to text Cecilia.

"Hey."

I set my phone on the stand by my bed and laid down with my feet kicked up on an extra pillow at the end of the bed.

My phone buzzed. I looked. It was her.

"Good morning," she wrote. *"How is everything?"*

"Great. Dad's home," I said.

"Good. I'm glad."

"How's work?" I asked.

"It's going. Are you working today?"

"No, but I do tomorrow. The head cook is leaving soon. I'm actually taking his position in another week. I'm kind of nervous about that. A lot of pressure to do well."

"You'll do fine. I believe in you."

"Thanks!"

I put the phone next to me and turned over. My eyes grew heavy.

2

I must have slept a few hours. I woke up at one o'clock in the afternoon. I didn't mean to. But I was so tired from everything. I got up and made my way into the living room. No one was there. I looked into dad's room and Marcus was sitting next to dad's bed watching him sleep. I felt a weight on my chest. I know my brother hadn't been around the last three years. Maybe he felt guilty? Did he have regrets? I didn't know. I could never know unless he told me, and this wasn't the time to ask. I closed the door softly, but not all the way. I left a crack and stepped away.

I went back to my room and sent a text to Cecilia.

"Any plans tonight? I have work all day tomorrow, but I'd really like

to see you this evening if you want."

I climbed back into bed. I was so drained from the past few days events that I wanted nothing more than to just lay and rest. My phone went off. I picked it up and read Cecilia's message.

"Well," she said. *"There is this handsome man that I want to see later on today."*

I smiled.

"Oh, yeah?" I wrote. *"Maybe he can take you to dinner?"*

"I would love that."

"Great! Meet me at the Ol' Burger House at seven o'clock."

"Okay," she said.

I closed my eyes again and drifted away.

3

I woke up to Marcus calling to me softly from my door.

"Yeah?" I said. My eyes barely open.

"Are you hungry?" he asked.

I turned over. "I have plans with a friend later. What time is it?"

"It's almost six o'clock."

"Oh, shit!" I got up quickly. "I need to shower!"

"A date?" Marcus asked.

"Not that it matters to you," I said, picking out clothes in my closet. "But yeah, something like that."

"I'm not trying to pry," Marcus said. "It was just a question."

"Oh? Now you care?" I got defensive. My tone was harsh and I wasn't letting up on my older brother. He had abandoned us and I was unforgiving. I didn't care much for him now. Just because he came back—just because he took the week off—it didn't matter to me much. I was cold and bitter—resentful.

"I'm just trying to— "

"What?" I said. "You're trying to do what exactly?"

"Sam," he said.

I could tell by the look on his face—that despair and hurt written all over it—that I had hurt him. It wasn't my intent. But I did want him to feel—I wanted him to feel like I did. I wanted him to feel alone in this world without hope. I wanted him to feel lost just like me. I was helpless these days, and I wanted him to experience that. He was my brother, but I wanted to cut into him like a knife.

He lowered his head and left the room. I continued looking through my closet not looking back. I stopped.

That was harsh, Sam.

I grabbed a pair of jeans and a nice shirt and headed for the shower.

Once I was finished in the bathroom, I put on my socks and shoes, sprayed some cologne, and headed out the door without a *goodbye* to Marcus. I figured dad was asleep, so I didn't say anything to him either. Plus, I didn't want to speak to Marcus right now. I wanted to have a good night with Cecilia. I certainly didn't want to meet her in a bad mood. So I left.

4

I got to the Ol' Burger House on time. Cecilia was in front of her car waiting for me. She looked wonderful. But her hair was different. Instead of red with blond bangs, it was now a dark purple.

"I love it," I said, as I approached her.

"Huh?"

"The hair." I pointed at her head.

"Oh, yeah," she said, and laughed. "Thanks!"

"Ready to go in?"

"Yes."

I opened the door for her and we entered. There was a little crowd *for a Monday*. But it wasn't overbearing. My anxiety would comply.

The hostess was a small, blond who looked to be in her early twenties.

"For two?" she asked.

I said, "Yes," and Cecilia gave a nod.

"Great," she said. "Follow me!"

We followed to a nice little table in the back corner of the restaurant with low lighting and a great ambiance. The music wasn't too loud and the conversations amongst the rest of the patrons were at a low volume. Ol' Burger House wasn't classy, but it was nicer than some of the other restaurants in town.

"What are you going to get?" I asked Cecilia.

"I'm not sure," she said, as she flipped through the menu. "Yourself?"

"Maybe one of their classic burgers. I'm thinking." I took my eyes off the menu and looked at her. I grinned.

She was beautiful. She had piercings and tattoos. I liked that. But the shape of her eyes and her soft lips were what captivated me. The shape of her face and chin complimented one another.

She looked up at me and said, "What?"

"I'm just admiring," I replied.

"Whatever." She laughed. "I'm getting the chicken fried steak."

"Good choice."

She looked back down at her menu.

A moment later, the waitress came and we placed our order. She walked away to put our order into the computer POS system.

"So …" Cecilia said.

I looked at her. "Yes?"

"No. Never mind."

I laughed. "What is it?"

"I was going to ask about your dad. I shouldn't though. It's none of my business."

"It's okay," I replied. "He's well. He's older, but the doctor said he's in good shape—but he does have to take it easy though for a while."

"Are you okay?" she asked, staring into my eyes.

"Yeah. It did scare me though when I found him. He was laying on the floor of our apartment."

"Oh, no!"

"Yeah—scared me half to death. I thought— well, you know."

"I'm glad he's fine now," she said.

She reached across the table and put her hand on the back of my hand. I followed her arm up to her gentle smile and soft stare.

"Thank you."

5

Now, we were eating our food. She had ordered the chicken fried steak and I *had* gotten a regular burger with cheese. The food was good and I was enjoying spending time with Cecilia. She had a way of making me feel comfortable around her. She was soft-spoken and easy-on-the-eyes. She didn't curse hardly and she *always* had something to say or had a response to everything I said — not once was I bored with the conversation. She was more than I could have ever asked for.

"Do you work tomorrow?" she asked me.

"Yeah. I've got to go back to the restaurant in the morning, and I work the second job as well."

"Long days," she sighed.

"For sure," I replied.

We ate most of our food but go to-go boxes for the last of it.

We were finished and I was paying when a group of guys walked by.

"Cecilia?" one of them said.

"Hey, Troy!" She lit up.

I was immediately concerned, and I guess I was jealous too. I felt hot. I wasn't sure if I was sweating. I didn't want to wipe my brow, but it felt moist.

She stood up and gave him a hug.

"How have you been?" he asked her. He was all smiles.

"Good!" She looked back at me. "This is my friend, Sam."

I was surprised she introduced me. She didn't have to. We had hardly gone out and I was really no one to Cecilia — I wanted to be, but we weren't at that point yet.

He extended his hand and I took his grip and shook it.

"I'm Troy," he said. "Nice to meet you, Sam."

He was tall and handsome — dirty blond and a killer grin — I couldn't compare. He was significantly more handsome than myself.

Was he an ex of hers?

"We were just leaving," Cecilia said. She waved at me insinuating I stand up, so I did.

"Well, it was good to see you, Cece," he said.

They hugged one final time and he walked away. She looked at me and rolled her eyes.

"An old friend," she said, then took up her to-go box. "Ready?"

I nodded, then followed her out of the restaurant. We walked passed the bar and said, "Thank you," as we exited.

"Who was that?" I asked, outside.

"Nobody," she replied. She kept on her way to her car.

"Uh-huh."

She stopped and turned to me. "He's just some guy I use to see last year."

"I figured. He seemed real happy to see you." There was a snide tone in my voice that I couldn't help. I was almost sarcastic. I hadn't dated in so long that I was immediately jealous when he said Cecilia's name. I couldn't help it.

"Sam," she said. "It's not a big deal. I broke up with him."

"Yeah. Save it."

What's wrong with me?

My paranoid, schizophrenic mind went to it's deep depths of loathing. I walked passed Cecilia and headed to my car.

"Sam!" she cried out.

I ignored her, opened up my car, and climbed in. The window was up. I heard her muffled cries, but I continued to brush her off and pulled out of the parking space. In my delusions, I figured they would get back together— I was only temporary. I had been *played.* I was only a *toy* for her to distract herself from Troy.

Fuck that!

I drove off and headed home. I gripped the wheel tight.

I can't believe I thought anything would happen with Cecilia. She clearly liked Troy. What's wrong with me?

I hit the wheel with a fist. My eyes swelled with tears. I was heartbroken.

18

Chapter 18

1

The next day at work, I was quiet.

I had to do both jobs today— Open House Bar and Grill *and* Mama Vici's.

Why did I act like that? Was I right? Or was I wrong for brushing off Cecilia?

I tried to get through my shift at the Open House as best as I could. Terry tried to talk to me, but I wasn't much for conversation. I was legitimately hurt by Cecilia. But was I wrong for getting jealous and upset? I tried not to think too much on the matter. I just wanted the day over with.

After the Open House, I went to Mama Vici's. My mood was a little better. It was five o'clock and I was prepping for the dinner rush. I made pasta, readied marinara sauce, and stocked the cheeses. My favorite thing to make there was the pizzas, although I had no previous experience with them.

The waitress, Caroline, was my opposite for the evening. There was her, myself, and the hostess.

Caroline was a curvy, short brunette. She had big eyes complimented with big eyelashes. I'm sure they were fake, but they looked nice on her. She was dark— dark hair and dark eyes. But her lips were red as an apple. She was pretty. But Cecilia was on my mind still that whole night.

"Table three ready?" Caroline asked me.

"Almost," I replied, through the food window of the kitchen.

There were two chicken Alfredo and one chicken Parmesan. I was hurrying to get out the order— I wanted all of the orders out quickly— I just wanted the day to be over.

About eight o'clock, it started to slow down. Caroline walked to the back where I was.

"Good job, Sam," she said.

I hadn't worked with her much in my time at Mama Vici's, but I was interested in talking to her.

Maybe Cecilia isn't the one?

"Thanks," I replied. "I try."

She giggled. "Well, you do well. I like working with you. You keep up and don't crack under pressure— a great cook."

I smiled, and she walked away.

Forget about it. She doesn't like you. Cecilia doesn't like you either.

I finished my shift. I clocked out and headed to my car. Caroline was parked next to me and she was walking close behind me.

"Sam!" she hollered.

I turned.

"I'll see you tomorrow?"

"Yeah," I replied.

"Great. Bye!"

She got into her car and left.

I stood there for a moment. It was cool out. It was eleven o'clock and the moon's light was subtle on the ground. Streetlights lit the sidewalks and only one car drove by. It was a ghost-town. Main Street was empty all except for myself. I got into my car, started it, and pulled away from Mama Vici's to head home.

2

I walked into the apartment. Dad and Marcus were sitting on the couch watching television.

"Hey!" dad said, his speech muffled by his oxygen mask.

126

"Hey, Sam," my brother greeted.

"Feeling better, dad?"

"Loads," he replied.

"Good," I said. "Long day." I walked passed the bar after throwing my keys down. "I'm headed to bed."

"Night," Marcus said.

I walked into my room and kicked off my shoes. I needed a shower, but I was mentally *and* physically exhausted. I just wanted to sleep, so I took off my shirt and laid down. I closed my eyes and saw Cecilia.

As I lay there thinking, Caroline popped into my head. Her long, dark hair down her shoulders.

I bet it smells good. She smells good from a distance— she had nice perfume on this evening.

I laid in bed and drifted off to sleep thinking of both Cecilia and Caroline. I felt better than earlier at the day's start.

I must have had my phone still in my pocket. I felt it vibrate. I looked and it was Cecilia— a text.

"I hope you're not mad at me. Are you upset?"

I laid my phone on my chest and thought for a moment.

Am I upset? How do I feel? I do like Cecilia. But why did that Troy *guy call her "Cece"? Cecilia had mentioned they saw each other last year. How serious was it? I guess he wasn't heartbroken enough to not say, "Hi!" Was I being an idiot?*

"Hey," I wrote back.

"What's wrong?"

"I don't know. Just seemed like you were happy to see Troy."

"I was being nice."

"Yeah."

"Don't be an asshole, Sam."

"I'm not. I'm just being myself."

"You're being ridiculous right now. I can't get through to you. You're a jerk!"

"Whatever," I replied, then tucked my phone beneath my pillow.

I don't need this grief. Screw her.

For the rest of the night, I had trouble sleeping. I tossed and turned as I thought of Cecilia.

Was I being an asshole? No! You're in the right!

I thought of Caroline.

Maybe she would be better for me. I'll see you tomorrow.

I finally fell asleep.

3

I woke up. It was two in the morning. There was yelling coming from the living room. It sounded like Marcus.

"No. Fuck you!" he screamed.

I got up out of bed and made my way to the living room.

"What's going on?" I asked.

"Fuck you. Fuck you!"

He was yelling into his cell phone.

"I don't have to put up with you lousy motherfuckers. I quit!" he screamed.

He threw his phone onto the couch and paced back and forth. He pushed his fingers through his hair.

"What the hell, Marcus?"

"They pushed me, Sam. They really pressed my buttons!"

He was furious. His face was red and stiff. Lip curled and teeth showing— almost snarling.

"So, you quit?"

Marcus paused. "I guess I did." He started to laugh. "I've been with them for *two years!* Jesus, what did I just do? Fuck that! My boss is a prick!"

"Are you going to be okay?" I asked.

"I guess." He started to pace again. "I guess I'm here for a bit too, now— longer than a week." He looked at me. "— if you need me that is."

"Yeah," I said. "Of course. You're welcome here, Marcus. Stay as long as you need. Dad needs you and I could use the help. He's a lot some times."

He laughed. "I'm surprised I didn't wake him up."

"Yeah, me too."

"Are you headed back to bed?"

"I'm kind of awake now," I replied. "You were loud as shit."

"Sorry."

4

I went in to work and all was quiet. All the staff was gathered at the bar. We weren't open yet.

"What's going on?" I approached my coworkers.

"It's Terry," Jessica said. "He was hurt last night."

"What do you mean?" I asked.

She sighed. "He was leaving the bar and he was mugged. The thief stabbed him."

"Jesus."

Greg walked over and put a hand on my shoulder.

"Is he going to be okay?" I looked at Greg.

"He's in the Intensive Care Unit," Greg said. "I'm sure he'll pull through. I know you two are close. If you need to take the day off, I'm sure Emilio will understand."

"No. I'm okay," I replied. "I'll be fine. I'm just worried now. My dad was just in the hospital."

"I know. It's a lot for you. If you *do* need to leave, it's fine," Greg reassured.

I walked away and to the back kitchen. I went to the dry-storage where I could be alone. I started to cry.

The tears ran down my face.

First dad, now Terry. What the fuck is going on?

I was feeling frustrated and overwhelmed. I hit my face with a fist on my cheek until the pain became just a numb feeling on my cheek muscles.

Maybe I should leave? You're stronger than this! Stay!

I wiped my face and went to the paper towel dispenser in the kitchen to blow my nose. I was calm now.

Greg walked into the kitchen. "It's okay, Sam."

I turned to him. "Fuck that! Fuck all this shit!" I slammed my foot on the ground. "It's not fair."

I started to cry again. Harder this time. Greg put his big arms around me and held me like a small child. I wept into his shoulder— tears, snot, and all. I'm sure it was the most vulnerable he had ever seen me. I was weak at the knees.

He pulled away from me.

"Go home, Sam. Go."

I nodded and headed to clock out.

19

Chapter 19

1

I pulled up to the hospital— the same one dad was just at. I wanted to see my friend. I *had* to make sure he was okay. I didn't want to lose him. Truth was: I didn't have many people I was close to. After I lost mom, I desperately wanted to keep everyone in my life. It was hard— losing loved ones; It was a part of life, I suppose. But, that didn't mean I had to endure the pain of loss.

I sat in my car and looked at myself in the rear-view mirror.

Not again. Not Terry.

I left the car and made it to the front lobby.

"I'm here to see Terry Matthews."

She looked at me and then her screen. The nurse said, "He can't be seen right now. He's still in ICU and we can't accept visitors. Unless you're family— are you kin to Matthews?"

"Well, no."

I should have said, "Yes."

"But he's a close friend," I said. "We're *like* brothers."

"I'm sorry, sir. You can't see him."

I put my hands onto the counter. I scoffed.

"I just want to see him," I replied.

"I'm sorry. Sir, maybe tomorrow."

"Tomorrow is too late." I slammed my fist on the counter. I was getting riled up. I slammed my foot on the tile.

"Sir, calm down."

"I just want to see him!"

"Security!"

A tall, goon walked up to me wearing a patch on his shirt that said: SECURITY.

"What the fuck do you want?" I yelled at him.

"Sir," he said. "You need to settle down."

He placed his hands on top of my shoulders, but I pushed them off.

"Fuck you!" I screamed. "I want to see my friend!"

He grabbed me by the arm.

"I want to see my friend!"

He escorted me out of the building.

"Not today, sir," he said, firmly, and tossed me to the ground.

I immediately got up and ran for the lobby door. He pushed off of me and threw me back to the ground.

"Son," he said. "You need to leave. Before I call the police."

"I want to see my friend! Terry! Terry!" I began to yell in front of the hospital's entrance. "Terry!"

"Calm down!" the security guard hollered at me.

He grabbed me again by the arm. "Where's your car, sir?"

"No! Terry!" I kept on, and kept on. I was hysterical.

"I've had it with you," he said. "I'm calling the police."

I kept pushing against him and yelling.

He took out his phone and dialed 9-1-1 because ten minutes later, the police were on scene.

"What's going on today, sir?" one officer asked me, his hands on his belt.

I was breathing hard and trying to calm myself at this point.

"Nothing," I replied. "I just wanted to see my friend, and this asshole won't let me."

"Right," he said. His partner looked at him. "What's going to happen now is you're going to come with us. We can't let you leave the premises alone. You've caused a scene and you're in our custody now."

I lowered my head.
Good going.

2

The officers walked me into the back of the police station.

"Follow me," one said.

I was handcuffed and his partner had me by the arm. We walked in and they took off my cuffs.

"Empty your pockets into the basket," he said.

I took out my phone, keys, and cigarettes and placed them into the small, white basket. They began to fingerprint me— thumbs to my pinky fingers.

"When you're in the cell—," he said. "Don't rub your eyes. There's no sink for you to wash your hands, but trust me— the ink burns if in your eyes."

I nodded. He walked me in front of a long, blue backdrop.

"We're getting your picture," his partner said. "Look at the camera."

I looked at the lens with a straight face. There was a small flash. After that, they walked me to the holding tanks.

"One of us will come grab you when you're time is up," the officer said.

If I had to guess, it was around noon. I had no idea how long they would keep me. I walked into the tank. He closed the large steel door behind me. I looked around. There was only a toilet and an L-shaped steel bed or seat— depending if a person wanted to lay or sit. I sat for a moment, then I eventually laid down. I closed my eyes and hoped I'd be released soon.

3

"Williams," I heard a voice call out from the entrance of the tank.

I opened my eyes and sat up.

"Samuel, you're free to go. Your brother is here."

I got up and walked out. The officer escorted me through the station and to the front lobby.

"Sam. Jesus. Are you okay? Greg from your work called me. They had heard you caused some kind of *scene* at the hospital this morning. What were you thinking?" Marcus said.

"I'm schizophrenic. I don't think— sometimes," I replied, while wiping my eyes. "Shit. The ink."

4

We were riding in the back of a taxi. It smelled of old soda and potato chips— had a stale and thick air to the cabin.

"I told the cab driver to go to the hospital so you can get your car," my brother said, looking at me.

"Thanks."

"Sam, I know you were distraught, but you can't do things like that."

I looked out the window, my hand on my chin.

"Are you listening?" he asked.

"Yeah, yeah. Be a *good boy* and *don't do drugs.* Got it."

"Sam, I'm serious."

"Why do you care now? You don't know me anymore— we're strangers."

"We're brothers."

"Hardly," I replied.

We pulled up to the hospital.

I said to the driver while pointing, "That's me right there."

He pulled over next to my car and I got out of the cab.

"Sam, we need to talk," my brother said.

I slammed the door in his face and walked away.

5

As I drove home, I thought about my life—everything was falling apart. Cecilia hated me, dad was sicker than ever, work was okay, and Terry had been hurt. Life had certainly given me plenty of lemons and there was no lemonade to be made.

I kept thinking I should text Cecilia, but I hadn't. Something told me not to. Something held me back from sending a simple, *"Hey."* I was torn between my feelings and my thoughts of self-doubt.

Dad was getting older, and my hero was fading before my eyes with each coming day. He use to be strong, but now he was a brittle old man.

I couldn't help an overbearing sadness wash over me. It consumed me like the darkness takes the light when nightfall hits. I couldn't explain what I felt if anyone were to ask—not that anyone *would*. I had few friends—and my best friend was hurt. I knew Terry was reckless, but how could he be so stupid to get mugged and hurt like that. He shouldn't have left the bar alone.

It's not his fault.

The tears in my eyes swelled again as I drove through town. My knuckles were white as I gripped the steering-wheel tightly. I twisted my grip on it to feel something. My hands hurt, but I wanted the pain. The tears rolled down my eyes and they made it hard to see.

It'll be okay. Everything will work out.

As I was crying, I didn't realize that I began drifting into the opposite lane. A car came at me and was honking.

"Jesus!" I yelled, and suddenly pulled the wheel to the right.

My car jerked back to the proper lane. My heart was pounding.

"I need to settle down," I whispered to myself.

I finally made it home.

I got out and slowly walked up to my apartment. The concrete steps were hard and lifeless. The echoes from my shoes hitting them sounded throughout the apartment complex walls. The metal railing was cold. The steel in my hand felt nice. I ran my hand across it as I went up.

At the door, I found the apartment key and let myself in.

Marcus stood there. He was waiting for me.

20

Chapter 20

1

"We need to talk," my brother, Marcus, said to me, as soon as I walked into the apartment.

"I really don't want to chat right now, man," I said.

"It's important."

"What?" I said, sternly.

Marcus looked at me. "A friend is getting me a job where he works. He's getting my foot in the door."

"Okay?"

"I have to leave the day after tomorrow."

"You said—"

"I know—I know I said I'd be here for the week or more, but I have to go, Sam."

"You're such an asshole," I yelled. I pushed passed my brother and headed for my room.

I tried to shut the door, but Marcus caught the edge and stopped me.

"I'll come back," he said.

"Oh, right. Yeah, we'll need you in another three years."

I couldn't believe Marcus. How could he be so selfish? He was leaving us—again.

My brother wasn't always like this—so caught up in his own *bullshit* that he couldn't see passed himself. He used to be caring—someone I looked up to. But mom's passing changed him. It had made him cold. It had made him selfish. It had made him blind to reality. We needed him, but, yet again, he was running away.

Marcus held onto the door. I was pushing trying to close it.

"Fuck off," I said.

"What's going on?" dad said, as he made his way slowly out of his room.

"Marcus is fucking leaving again," I told him.

"Dad, it's just for a little bit."

"Son. Marcus, you two settle down."

I kept pushing on the door. "Let go!" I hollered.

"No," Marcus yelled back.

At this point, he had half his body blocking the doorway.

"Son! Let him shut the door," dad said. His words muffled beneath the oxygen mask.

"He's being a child," Marcus said, back to dad. "I have things that I have to take care of and Sam is in *La la land.*"

"Fuck you, man!" I kept pushing on the door trying to get Marcus out of the way. I had one hand on the door and the other on Marcus. "Let go!"

"Boys, you both need to quit!"

Dad stumbled backwards.

"Boys—"

He collapsed onto the couch.

I saw dad fall. "Dad!" I opened the door and Marcus fell forward. I hopped over him and ran into the living room. "Marcus, you prick! You hurt dad."

Marcus got up and ran back. We were both by dad's side. He was panting underneath his oxygen mask holding onto his chest.

"I'm okay, I'm okay," he was saying gently.

His head was tilted upwards as if looking at the ceiling.

"Dad, I'm sorry," Marcus said.

I looked at my brother. "See. We still need you, you selfish *fuck.*"

Marcus looked at dad. "Should I call 9-1-1?"

"No," dad said. "I'm okay, boys. I'm okay."

He was still holding on to his chest, but his breathing slowed now. For a moment, we thought he was having another attack. Dad reassured us, however, that he was fine and didn't need to go to th hospital.

"Leave me be, boys," he said. "It's not an attack. I'm okay. I just got excited is all."

"Okay," I said.

"Take me to my room, Mark," he said, and grabbed onto my brother's arm.

"Yes, daddy," my brother said, and helped him to his feet.

They walked to my dad's room. Marcus got dad into bed and covered him with the blankets.

I looked from the living room.

"If you need anything—"

"Yes, yes. I know who to call," dad said, and smiled.

Marcus shut his door softly as he walked out.

"I'm sorry," my brother said, as he walked into the living room. "I didn't mean for that to happen. I just wanted you to know, Sam."

"I know, man. I know."

2

I sat with Marcus in the living room.

"I need a smoke," I said.

"Sam, you know I love you guys," he said, with sincere eyes gazing into mine. His face was soft and emotions genuine. I could tell he was truthful. He wasn't bullshitting.

"We love you too, man, and that's why I was hoping you would be in town for longer than a couple of days."

"I know, but I have to. I didn't plan it, I hope you know. It's an opportunity. I kind of *have* to. I have a life back in New York."

"Life sucks," I said. "Always has a way of beating you down."

"Don't say that."

"It's true."

I got up off the couch and walked out to the balcony. I lit up a cigarette, inhaled the smoke, and breathed out.

Just what I needed.

I felt my phone vibrate in my pocket. I took it out and looked. It was a text from Greg.

"Terry will be okay. Just have faith."

I stood there—cigarette in one hand, phone in the other—then I thought of Cecilia. I knew I liked her. I wanted her. I wanted her to be with me. I shouldn't let the other night bother me. I was being insensitive and I'm sure it was all a misunderstanding—mainly on my part.

Ah, fuck …

I wrote, *"Hey. How are you?"* and sent it to her.

I finished my smoke and went inside.

"So, when exactly are you leaving?" I asked Marcus, as I entered the living room from the patio.

"Thursday—early morning."

I nodded. "I can take you to the airport. I have work, but I can drop you off before."

"Thanks, Sam."

I headed for my bedroom. Before I got there, my phone went off.

3

"I've been thinking about you."

I was reading Cecilia's texts while laying in bed.

"I was worried," it said.

I looked at the screen—looked up at the ceiling—looked around the room.

Hmmm … What to say when you've been an ass?

"I'm sorry."

It was all I could think of to write. I waited, anticipating her response. I lay, with eyes shut, thinking of her face—how the light would touch upon it, her eyes were big and bright—I felt at peace.

Finally, my phone buzzed.

"It's okay," she said.

I smiled and lifted myself up. I propped the pillow up on the wall and sat against it.

"I miss you," I replied. *"It's hard for me to say the things I mean some times. I'm not very good at this kind of stuff. I've only had a few girl friends, and they never lasted long. My longest relationship was a little over a*

139

year. I really am sorry if I offended you. I didn't mean to accuse you of anything. I just—I really like you and my brain started over thinking. I'm a paranoid schizophrenic, so I guess that's where my head was at—in some paranoid part of my brain; I'm sorry."

"You're okay. I understand. I have anxiety and depression. It can be tough. I get it."

I felt better now. I could rest knowing Cecilia didn't hate me and that I didn't ruin everything.   I put my phone down on the night stand next to my bed and turned over on my side.

4

I wasn't sure what time it was when I opened my eyes, but there was barely any light coming in from the window; It wasn't dark outside totally. I sat up and grabbed my phone. It read "seven o'clock". I must have dozed off.

Cecilia had replied earlier and I was happy about that—I really did like her. I wanted things to work out with us. I didn't care about any other women. I had a feeling about her.—she was different and someone special. I felt like my heart grew three times its size when I had read her texts earlier. I wanted to see her.

"Do you want to meet?" I wrote.

I got out of the bed as I waited for a reply. I made my way to the living room. Only Marcus was there.

"Where's dad?" I asked.

"Resting. Sleeping."

Marcus had the television barely audible. It was the evening news—dad's favorite.

"I figured I'd keep this on in case he got up," Marcus said. "You know him—he loves current events."

I went for a glass of water.

My phone went *buzz, buzz*. I took it from my pocket and looked—it was Cecilia.

She wrote, *"I'd love to. But give me an hour?"*

"Perfect."

"Okay. I can't wait."

I put the phone away and turned to Marcus. "Book your flight out already?"

"Yeah. Everything is set. I start Monday."

"Same 'banking-stuff'?" I asked.

"Always." He grinned.

I had to hurry. I downed the glass of water and headed back to the room. I grabbed some fresh clothes and made my way to the shower. As I stood in the tub and let the water run over the back of my head, I saw Cecilia's smile in my mind—the way her lips would tilt, the shape of her mouth as she talked—I saw her vividly within my head.

I got out and dressed. I went to grab my keys on the kitchen counter.

"Leaving?" Marcus asked me.

"Yes. Going out with a friend."

"Girl friend?"

"Yeah."

"Good, Sam. You deserve somebody."

He smiled at me, folded his arms, and leaned back on the couch. "Love you, little brother."

I hesitated, but then replied, "I love you too, Marcus." I walked out of the apartment.

5

I walked to my car and got in. I took out my phone and pulled up the texts with Cecilia. I wrote, *"Meet at the Brewery Company."*

The sun was setting—burnt orange in the sky with purple riddled throughout. The blue backdrop was opposite of those vibrant colors—not a single cloud in the sky. I pulled out of my parking space and headed out.

When I got to the Brewery Company, I guessed that Cecilia hadn't arrived yet. I parked, got out, and leaned against my car. I scrolled through my social media as I waited. The anticipation hurt—I had made a fool of myself. Although Cecilia said I was okay, I still felt like a jerk. I was insensitive to her and I really was being an *asshole.*

At this time burnt orange turned to a deep red in the sky and blue hues of the fall turned to a purple blanket in the sky. There were a few stars peaking through—now, there were a few clouds scattered throughout, but, they too, were colored either purple or a navy blue.

As I looked up at the sky and admired the work of Him—Oh, how he could paint the sky each evening—I knew everything would be okay.

"Sam!" I heard a voice call out. I turned around and it was Cecilia. She waved an arm at me.

"Hey," I replied, and walked towards her.

She got close and hugged on me. It felt nice and I felt like I was home—a home before mom passed, dad got old, and Marcus left—where all would be just fine. Her warmth comforted me. She drew back.

"I missed you," she said, looking up at me. She slapped my chest. "Jerk!" She smiled.

"I'm sorry—again. I don't know why I acted like that. I just get in my own head some times, I guess."

"It's okay. But settle down—or talk to me next time. Don't just assume."

I nodded.

"Let's go in!" She took my hand and led me to the entrance.

21

Chapter 21

1

We sat at the bar. She was turned facing me with a hand on my leg. I tried not to look down, but I felt her touch and it drove me wild deep inside. She smiled and told me about her childhood. She mentioned sunflowers, bugs, middle school, childhood fears, and her parents.

"Yeah, my dad is my hero too," I told her, while looking deep into her eyes. The light from behind the bar bounced of her eyes and illuminated her gaze—she was wide-eyed and smiling. In this moment, I felt she was just for me—like I had been waiting my whole life to meet this woman—and here she is, at last; My angel was finally here. There *was* someone out in the world just for me—named *Cecilia*.

As I stared, I slowly started to lean in. I felt a magnetism between us, so I got close and waited for her to draw near and kiss me. She pressed her lips on mine. I didn't care that there were people around. I felt her warm kiss on me and a feeling of bliss washed over my body—it was like little soft pricks all over: in my legs, arms, back, and cheeks. I never felt this before—like I could fall into someone just by their very presence. I could fall into a dream that was made just for us two—it was a fantasy turned reality in a modern day play about two lovers and the hearts that had found each other after years of searching.

"I like you," I said, as I pulled away slowly from her kiss.

"I like you too."

She looked into my eyes—her's flickered from side to side.

She then asked me, "Do you want to come over?"

"To your place?"

"Yes."

"Okay."

She got up, I payed the bill, and we left for the parking lot.

Outside, she said," Follow me."

I got into my car and followed behind her as we headed for her apartment. My stomach turned and knots grew deep inside it.

2

We pulled up to her apartment complex. I got out. My mind was running a million miles-per-hour, but I tried to stay cool—or at least *appear* cool-headed.

"I'm on the third floor," she said, as she started for the stairs.

I followed.

We walked up the flight of stairs and said nothing to each other. We got to the third floor and walked down a corridor to the third door on the left.

"This is me," she said, with a smile. She took out her keys and opened the door.

I walked in and everything was so quaint. It smelled nice too—like flowers during the Spring time. Everything was organized and put up. There were family photos on the living room wall, a painting above the couch of a cabin in the woods, and her dining room table had nice, red place-mats with a vase.

"Sunflower," I said.

"Huh?"

I pointed to the vase. There was a single sunflower in it.

"Oh, yes," she smiled. "My mom gave it to me last week."

"I like it."

"Are you going to kiss me again or not?"

Cecilia looked up at me with a grin. I looked down at her. She

144

wrapped an arm around my neck. I leaned in and pressed my lips hard against hers. We kissed for a moment, then she walked me to her room.

The evening was wonderful and our bodies made *love* into the night.

As I lay in her bed and looked out the window, those few stars had turned into many in the dark purple and deep gray sky. Although I couldn't see the moon, it's light poured into her room and blanketed Cecilia's naked body. I caressed her with my fingertips— I ran them along her side as she lay down next to me.

"I like you a lot," she whispered, with eyes closed.

"Shhh—sleep."

After a moment, her breathing grew heavier. I got up, put on my jeans, and headed for the outside patio to grab a cigarette. I left the apartment and lit up my smoke. I could see the moon now. It wasn't full—not even half-way—but it was beautiful and bright. It illuminated the sky. I had heard once the moon didn't shine, it simply bounced the Sun's rays, but tonight, she certainly *did* shine—brighter than the Sun even.

I walked back inside.

Cecilia was asleep, so I got dressed and saw myself out. I locked the door behind and made my way down those flights of stairs to my car. I sat for a second.

"Thank you," I said a loud to whomever may be listening— some *higher* force floating around out there in the sky above.

I pulled away and headed for home.

3

I walked into my apartment and heard Marcus whimpering on the couch. He was sitting in the dark. I turned on the lamp next to the couch.

"Why are you crying?"

"Dad—he's not waking up, Sam," my brother replied, looking at me with swollen, teary eyes.

I was confused. I ran to dad's room and sat quickly next to him. I pushed against his body—it felt cold. "Dad!" I yelled. I shook him— again, and again—trying to wake him, but he wouldn't open his eyes.

145

His oxygen mask was on his face, yet there was no breath on it. I stood up and pulled on my hair. I started to cry. "Dad—"

"He's gone," my brother said, as he walked into the room.

I was hysterical.

Not dad, too …

"I called the ambulance, Sam. They're on the way."

"You can't take him! He's okay. He's okay!"

"Sam—"

"Fuck you, Marcus! This is what you wanted, so you wouldn't have to be responsible for anything."

I turned and shoved my brother.

"Fuck you, man!" I kept saying, over and over again until Marcus grabbed me and pulled me into his arms. He held onto me tightly.

"It'll be okay," he said, as I let out all of my tears into his shirt. "It'll be okay."

I couldn't believe that our dad was gone. All these years of being my hero and now he's gone.

"He's in a better place now, Sam," my brother said, as he combed my hair with his fingertips. "He's in Heaven now."

"I just want him here," I said, with my face buried in my brother's chest. "God, why?"

I was crying hysterically when the EMT's showed up. I was sitting on the couch, facing down at the floor, and holding myself. They took our father's body out of the apartment quietly.

In the wee hours of the morning, we watched our father go into the ether.

"I wasn't here," I managed to get out through my crying.

"Don't do that to yourself," Marcus replied. He put a hand on my shoulder. "There's no one to blame and you don't need to put that on yourself."

"I should have been here."

"I love you, Sam. We'll get through this."

22

Chapter 22

1

Three days later, we had the funeral for dad.

Dad was buried next to mom, like he wanted. They were together now. After three years, they had been reunited.

I stood there and looked down at his casket as it was lowered into the plot. Tears ran down my face as I was beside my brother.

Dad didn't have much family—one younger sister that said she couldn't make it from Arkansas. It was okay. Dad had us—his two beloved sons. I was never sure how Marcus felt about dad—if he thought of him as a *hero* like I did. But watching him weep softly while dad was laid to rest reassured me that he thought of him unconditionally and that Marcus's leaving was for a purpose. I know my brother never meant to hurt us—he did me—but I knew deep down that dad never resented him for it. Dad understood—dad was always understanding.

After the funeral, we stood by my car. There was an overcast this day. It was gray outside and somewhat dark for eleven in the morning.

"Thought you were leaving," I said.

"Thought you were straight," my older brother replied, teasing.

We both laughed.

"I was supposed to—"

"I know. I'm just kidding."

"But I'll start the new job Monday."

"You're sticking around?"

"Yeah. Don't want to leave you alone in all of this."

I looked at my brother, then hugged him softly. "Thanks, Marcus. You're a good big brother—and although I was mad at you for a long time, I'm not anymore. I know dad wouldn't hold a grudge, so neither should I."

"I love you," he said to me.

"I love you too."

We got into the car and headed for home.

2

It's funny how life works—you live, work, raise kids—then you *die.* I understood the process, even though I didn't like it. God is mysterious, but his sense of humor sure can be sick at times.

I had told Cecilia about dad's passing that morning when I thought she might be awake after we slept together three days ago. She gave me her condolences, said she was sorry, and if I needed anything that she was there for me. I appreciated that.

My brother and I walked into my apartment lost—two kids grown without a father now. It would be hard, but I know we will manage.

"Don't be a stranger," I said, as I threw the keys onto the bar.

"You too," Marcus said. "You too."

About the Author

Branson M. Smith is local to South Texas, Ingleside specifically. He's an aspiring writer and poet. He was born in 1989 and grew up with a love of reading and writing. His stories were inspired by the movies he would watch as a young boy. He's a graduate of Ingleside High School class of 2007. He attended Del Mar College in Corpus Christi, Texas for a few semesters as an English major. After a five-year hiatus, he is back to writing and doing what he loves, besides guitar and music. For more information on the author, visit: www.officialbransonsmith.com, or find him on Facebook @bransonsmithwriter

Other Titles:

Natural Things: poems
Absence: new poems

Excerpt from Smith's new project: "The Disappearance of Cassandra Pruitt"

Josh pulled up to his parent's house and parked next to his mom's SUV. His dad's truck was in the street next to the curb. All was quiet as he got out of the car.

His mom came out of the house with eyes full of tears. They were red and swollen. She immediately grabbed onto him with both arms and wrapped him up as if he was a child in a warm blanket.

"Son—"she said.

"Mom, why didn't you guys tell me sooner about this?"

"The police said not to worry. That they had everything handled— we thought she would be home by now."

"Jesus."

"We're so scared something has happened to her, Josh. I don't know what to do. Your father will barely say two words."

"Dad needs to be strong," Josh said. "We'll find her. I promise." He wiped his mother's eyes.

"Come in," she said. "Alex is watching TV, and your dad is in the kitchen with his coffee. Do you want a cup?"

"I guess, mom. Let's go inside."

Josh escorted his mom inside the house.

"Dad?" Josh asked, aloud.

His father was quiet, sipping at his coffee in the kitchen. He sat up high at the bar. He was on a tall barstool that made his dad look short.

The air was warm inside—warmer than in his car. His little brother, Alex, who was four, sat in the living room watching his cartoons. His mom stood next to his father.

"What have the police said or done?" Josh asked.

"Well— "his mom said.

"They haven't done *shit,* " his dad replied. "They haven't done a *God-damn thing,* son!" He stood up from the stool. "Is that what you came up here for, Josh." His dad was becoming angry. "Is that why you're here? Cassandra is gone—*gone*— and she's not coming *home.* " He threw his coffee cup across the kitchen, and it broke on the wall. Josh's little brother started to cry hysterically from the living room. "She's gone, Josh! Is that what you want to know?"

His mother put her hands on his dad's shoulders. "Terry, calm down," she screamed.

"You calm down, Lisa! My little girl is gone, and no one knows where the fuck she is!"

"Dad," Josh hollered.

"Don't *'dad'* me, you little shit. You've always been the worst one. Why wasn't it *you?* Fuck you, Josh! You're no help to this family, and you've never been shit!"

"Dad," Josh said, once again. "I'm only here to help."

"Yeah! Okay!" his dad hollered. "Some help! A high-school drop-out cook. Yeah, thanks for saving the day, son! Such a big *help!"*

"Terry," his mom yelled. "You need to settle down right now! That's my boy."

"Oh, Lisa, don't give me that 'first-born' shit! He's a loser and doesn't do this family any good!"

"He's your son," she screamed.

"He ain't *shit* to me. He's some stranger."

"Well, fuck you, dad," Josh simply whispered, and headed for the front door. "I'll see you, Alex," he said, as he left his parent's house.

Only come to help and I get all this shit!

His mother ran out after him.

"Son," she yelled. "Come back!"

Josh stopped and turned. "I know dad's always been an *asshole,* but I didn't deserve that."

"I know. Just stay. Please." His mother's eyes swelled once again. "He'll come around. Your dad is just hurting, son"

"Yeah. I get that all too well."

"He loves you, Josh."

"I don't think so." Josh stood quiet for a moment. "If he'll settle down, I'll come back in. I want to know about Cassandra—what the cops know—I need to know what's going on. Her and I have always been close. You know that, mom."

His mom nodded. "Okay. I'll talk to him." She went back inside.

Josh stood and smoked two cigarettes exactly before his mom came back outside.

"Come in," she said.

He began to walk back up to the house where he grew up in. He looked at his mom before he entered. "If he starts his shit, I'm leaving."

"I know," she replied.

Made in the USA
Columbia, SC
12 March 2024

32498459R00088